# A PROMISE FULFILLED

## A TWEEDE KANS COVE CHRISTMAS

### DUBOIS-ARAZI FAMILY NOVELS
### BOOK ONE

## UNOMA NWANKWOR

KEVSTEL PUBLICATIONS

First printing December 2019

Printed in the United States of America

www.kevstel.com

*To my husband Kevin, and my kids—Fumnanya & Ugo.
Their support is immeasurable.*

# ACKNOWLEDGMENTS

To my Lord and Savior Jesus Christ. I thank you for paying the ultimate price that I may have life and for your grace which I do not deserve. Thank You for the gift of writing and I humbly pray I continue to be a vessel in this journey.

To my family, my husband Kevin who's my number one fan, cheering me along every step of the way. I love you and thank you. To my kids Fumnanya and Ugo, my gang, my pookies, my munchkins who keep me sane when insanity sometimes abound. I love you both more than words can express. I pray for God's continued protection over you.

To my parents and mother in-law, *Daalu*. Thank you for your constant prayers and speaking words of life, courage and hope upon me.

To my readers, author friends and sistah writers thank you, thank you. Sometimes support doesn't always come from the people or places you expect but trust in God and He will send the right people to you.

# NOTE FROM THE AUTHOR

The last time you heard from me, I was closing out the Sons of Ishmael series with A Danjuma story of the brothers' baby sister, Halima. Normally I wouldn't release another book so soon, but I haven't given my readers a Christmas story in about seven years.

So, I'm excited to introduce a brand-new family during Christmas. With this release, I'm starting something new.

Drum roll...the setting is in my first FICTIONAL town, Tweede Kans Cove. This town, although fictional, borders the real city it was mirrored after: Ifrane. The cultures and traditions are based on facts although a little loose. There's enough given in the book that will ground you, however, I highly suggest you go to my website (https://unomanwankwor.com/books/tweedes-kans-cove/) and read about the town.

Exciting things are happening in the U. N Universe. We're turning a new decade and a lot of things will be leveled up. I pray you join me for the ride.

Now to this new family. The DuBois-Arazis of Tweede Kans Cove are French Moroccans. I got first hand feedback that they are an awesome bunch. They are well explained in the book, however, you can also find out some in-depth information about them on my website. (https://unomanwankwor.com/books/tweedes-kans-cove/)

As usual, if you have additional questions you can reach me at www.unomanwankwor.com

Several readers loved the enunciations and translations, so they have been included in this book also. I might continue the trend.

Be blessed and I hope you enjoy Yasmine & Kojo's story, the first book in the DuBois- Arazi family novels. This my dear reader is a new beginning.

Unoma

# PRAISE FOR THE UNOMA NWANKWOR

"Whew! Unoma's characters were so real. They were honest, flawed, vulnerable, stubborn and saved by grace. I love when Unoma uses Africa as the backdrop for her romantic settings. Her spiritual message was clear: God's mercy and grace. Look out the Jamieson men, the Danjuma Brothers have arrived!!!" ~ **Pat Simmons, Award-winning author of the Guilty Series.**

"I love how Unoma Nwankwor weaves the distinctive, spicy flavor of West Africa into her novels. I feel right at home with the food, pidgin English, quirky expressions, and cultural norms. I'm also enjoying watching her grow as an author. ~**Sherri L. Lewis, Bestselling Author and Missionary**

Nwankwor adds more depth with the cultural nuances that could be a roadblock or a gateway to understanding. She expertly intertwines all of these elements, including faith lessons, to make a tightly woven story for a reader's enjoyment. ~ **USA Today Review of An Unexpected Blessing.**

"Unoma's writing reads effortlessly. There is the perfect infusion of faith and international flavor. Readers are quickly swept up on a romantic literary adventure. **The Christmas Ultimatum** is a great read for anytime of the year" ~ **Norma Jarrett Essence Best Selling author of Sunday Bruch**

"**When You Let Go** is a true testament of the power of God within ourselves and our marriage. Although, we are tested every day, it is up to us to lean on our faith to get through those difficult times and offer forgiveness to those who may have hurt us in the process. Amara and Ejike's faith was tested throughout this novel but once they learned to put God at the forefront of their household, they were able to weather the storm." ~ **Diva's Literary World**

*2* 001

With his arm draped around her neck, he led them along the coastline. It was Friday early evening, and they had just seen *My Date with the President's Daughter* at the Kans Cinema House. Sci-fi was more his speed, but considering the news he had to break to her, he let her have her way. He was grateful she didn't ask him any questions because he was asleep for most of the movie.

The silence that enveloped them was welcomed as he let the confessions of a couple of minutes ago sink in. He felt her shiver and readjusted his jacket over her shoulders. He wasn't sure if her chilled reaction was from the cold of the night or the residue of the tears she had shed.

He guided them toward the large rock at the mid-point of the path. Leaning against it, he drew her in between his legs.

"Come on, stop crying. It's not the first time you've gone on holiday with your family."

"But this is the first time you're not going with us," she sniffled. "Christmas is ruined."

He lifted his thumb and wiped the tear that was cascading down her cheek. Any time he saw her cry, his chest constricted. With her at sixteen and he two years her senior, people called what they had puppy love. But they, even at that age, knew their souls were connected.

"My uncle is coming down. Aren't you happy for me?"

Her hazel eyes met his. "Of course I am. How can you even ask that?" She hit his chest.

He chuckled. There was that fiery temper. Even though he didn't like that trait of hers, in this moment, he'd take it over her tears.

"Okay, calm down firecracker." He slid her hair behind her ears and kissed her forehead.

"I'll miss you. But I'll be right here when you get back," he reassured her. "Don't forget, I love you."

"I love and will miss you too. Promise me again."

"How many times tonight?"

"I like hearing it." She shrugged.

He'd do anything she wanted. He lifted her chin, looked into her eyes, and said, "One day, I'll make you my wife."

She giggled, and he tweaked her nose. "Come on, let me get you home. I don't want to have to beat your brothers again. One day they'll be my in-laws."

*Eighteen Years Later*

"You're on the run again?"

Yasmine DuBois-Arazi closed her eyes and reopened them to the sound of her grandmother's voice behind her.

"Okay, that's perfect. I'll call you back during the week to make the final arrangements." Yasmine disconnected the call, put on a smile, and turned to face Lady Olivia DuBois, or Grandma Olly as she and her siblings fondly called her.

"*Je t'aime aussi*, Grandma." Yasmine professed her love in French. She walked over to her and draped her arm around her shoulders. Her grandmother, who was the epitome of grace and elegance, took her hand and walked over to the teak swing on the other end of the massive porch.

Awkward silence loomed over them as her grandmother sat with her hands cupped in her lap. Her glasses lay perched on her straight nose, and her gaze fixed on the grounds of the DuBois Manor. Yasmine knew what her grandmother was going to say but still wanted her to go first. She tightened the sash of her sweater and admired the mini Christmas wonderland in front of her. Nobody in Tweede Kans Cove came close to Lady Olivia when it came to Christmas decorations. As with anything she did, it wasn't over the top, but classy and elegant. There wasn't any mistaking the fact that Grandma Olly and her landscaper put a lot of thought into the layout.

When she made it in earlier, Yasmine noticed the mailbox decorated with signature red and green flowers with a large bow. The half a mile-long driveway had an array of luminaries twinkling bright, and as usual, the shrubbery had garlands on them. The light snow that fell the previous evening gave the land the perfect white, fluffy overlay. The rest of the world would think it was Europe. But they were in good ol' Tweede Kans Cove right in the middle of the Atlas Mountains of Morocco in Northern Africa.

"Grandma, I love sitting here, looking at your decorations. As usual, they're amazing, but I'm kinda hungry. Can we go in now?" Yasmine's eyes darted from her grandmother to the front door that was adorned with a wreath displaying the DuBois family crest.

*All this and it's just November 26th. I have three more weeks 'till I'm out of here.*

"Yasmine Camille DuBois-Arazi, you *will* sit it out for however long it takes me to gather my thoughts and figure out where I went wrong with you." Her grandmother turned and looked at her with pursed lips and stern, blue eyes. Her olive skin was blemish and almost wrinkle-free, despite her being in her late sixties. If it weren't for her natural silver curls, she could pass for forty.

"What have I done this time, grandma?" Yasmine didn't want to disappoint her grandmother, but she was a thirty-four-year-old woman, and this was one situation where she couldn't please her.

"Why are you so bent on letting the past dictate your future?" her grandma asked.

Yasmine remained quiet because she knew her grandmother really wasn't expecting an answer. That question was just the segue into a conversation they'd had so many times, during this same time of the year...Christmas.

"That your parents and late husband were met with their unfortunate fates at this time of the year has nothing to do with you."

Yasmine's body stiffened. *Those weren't the only two events.*

She hated when people, especially her family, tried to belittle her feelings because they couldn't understand. She wasn't directly responsible for any of those bad memories, but they'd happened. She suffered emotionally as a result. The season reminded her of them, so she couldn't do Christmas. As simple as that.

"Grandma..."

The older woman took Yasmine's hand, pausing her speech. "*Écoute mon enfant.* When your grandpa and I got you and your siblings, it was my second chance. To do with the four of you what I somehow failed to do with my late daughter. I think I was too hard on her. For that reason, I've sat back for four years and watched you take my great-granddaughter and run far away from us during Christmas. I've had my say, but I didn't push. Christmas is a time for joy, hope and family."

She paused and tucked Yasmine's loose curl behind her ear. Then she continued, "She's six, she's just four years younger than you were when you came to live with me. Back then, I knew you needed love, stability and security and I've done my best to provide it for the four of you. You have the love part down, but the stability and security aren't there if you're not building traditions for her. Moving her from one place to another. I won't tell you how to raise Anisa..." She stood letting the last part of her lecture fade off. She kissed Yasmine's forehead.

"Remember, you'll never be truly happy if you keep trying to control everything. Now let's go eat. I'm sure your brothers and sister are tired of waiting."

"I'll be in in a minute, grandma," Yasmine said, her tone sober.

Her grandmother smiled, nodded and disappeared into the house.

Yasmine stared at the closed door. She should've listened to her sister, Salma, who advised her to wait until she got to her own cottage before she called the family pilot who was stationed in Marrakech. She needed to ensure that he was aware that he'd have to take her and Anisa to Nairobi on the twentieth and not the twenty-second of December, as she'd previously communicated. How was she to know her grandmother would be eavesdropping?

Now what her grandmother had said played in a loop in her head. Not the whole sermon about why she should leave the past in the past or about Christmas. Bad things happened during Christmas and she wasn't in the mood to celebrate. That was her truth and she was sticking to it...period.

However, the part about Anisa bothered her. Her daughter was her heart, the sole reason she existed. Unlike her mother, who chose a man – their father – over her and her siblings, she would always put Anisa's needs before her own. She was the only good thing that came out of her marriage to Pierre Chetrit.

"Mummy, Uncle 'Stafa said come on."

Yasmine smiled at her daughter peeking her head out of the door. She stood and walked over. Her daughter, with her olive skin, flowing curls, wide brown eyes and button nose was a replica of her late husband. She was the one thing Yasmine didn't regret about the union.

"Are you okay, Mummy?" Anisa asked, her forehead lined with concern.

Yasmine looked down at her and picked her up. "Yes, I am, my angel. Are you?"

"Yes, it's Christmas time," she yelled, wiggled down and took off down the foyer.

Grandma Olly's words played through her head again. However, her growling stomach paused the broken record, pushed her feet in motion and propelled her into the massive dining room.

*H*ours later, everyone was stuffed. As they did every Saturday for as far back as she could remember, Yasmine and her siblings sat in the family room of their grandparents' home. Unlike most families that had brunch on Sunday, they had theirs on Saturday. Sundays, their grandmother insisted they "take their blessings home."

"What's going on with the Hope for the Holidays program?" her older brother, Mustafa DuBois-Arazi asked, dividing his attention between her and Anisa, who had him wrapped up in a puzzle.

"From the last report I received, everything was going smoothly." Yasmine flipped through the fashion magazine in her hand. "How was Ghana?"

"Ghana was fine. The place is almost up and ready for you to descend on it," Mustafa replied.

But before Yasmine could ask of the details, her grandmother's voice took over. "What do you mean last report you received? Why are you not handling it personally?" Grandma Olly looked up from the blanket she was knitting and narrowed her eyes at her.

*Today is not my day.*

"Grandma, I have too much to do. But I assure you everything will be okay," Yasmine said.

"She's allergic to Christmas." Her younger brother Omar coughed, trying to hide his statement.

Yasmine shot him a stern look. He'd always taken exceptional pleasure getting on her nerves. She didn't have time to start explaining to her grandma that she wasn't trying to touch that event with a ten-foot pole. Hence, she only got weekly updates from her deputy manager.

"Yasmine, I don't need to tell you how important this is. I'm the Chair of the event. The church and Grand Amour—"

"Grandma, I've never let you down, have I?"

Grand Amour Spa & Resorts was the exclusive luxury resort she ran with her three siblings. The family-owned resort was co-hosting a "Hope for the Holidays" Christmas benefit to raise money for Beautiful Eyes, the town's orphanage and missions house. When their grandfather, Sir Marcelle DuBois, passed away five years ago, he handed over the reins to her older brother; Mustafa. He now served as the Chairman and Managing Director. Her younger brother, Omar, who was an award-winning chef, served as the Food & Beverage Director. And Salma, the baby of the group served as the Director of Guest Services and Activities.

As the General Manager & Director of Operations, Yasmine had to make sure everything ran smoothly. And she definitely had everything under control.

Her grandmother stared at her, but answered the only way she could, "Yes."

Yasmine knew she was apprehensive because she'd be leaving Tweedes for the holidays, but she would never let the family or Grand Amour Spa & Resorts down.

Her grandmother stared at her for a few more seconds. Comfortable with her answer, she went back to knitting while Yasmine threw a pillow at Omar, who was stretched out on the sofa watching television. He threw one back, nearly knocking over a vase.

Just like the outside of the house, festive ornaments adorned the DuBois home. The fireplace mantel held delicate, scented, pillar candles placed in gold crusted lanterns, ivory and gold jeweled stockings for each one of them and the words "Faith, Hope and Love" in red and white lettering wrapped in some garland. Even the smell of the place was Christmassy with her grandmother's traditional amber holiday simmer looming the air. Every week during the holidays, she'd have a simmering pot of cinnamon sticks, cloves, cranberries, vanilla extract, dried ginger, cardamom, star anise and her special amber paste essential oil.

"Are you guys done?" Mustafa asked, with his brow raised.

"*hal tasheur baltjahl*?" Omar countered in Arabic. "Are you feeling left out?"

Because of the way they spent their childhood, she and her siblings mainly communicated in English and Arabic; Berber to be exact. It wasn't until they moved to Tweedes that they learned French, which their grandparents predominantly spoke.

"No, but if you want to be out of five thousand dollars, be my guest."

"Grandma, tell me you didn't buy that vase for five thousand dollars?" Omar sat up. "That's over forty-eight thousand dirhams."

"It was a gift from your grandpa and mind your business," their grandma said.

Omar let out a hearty laugh. "It is my business because it's ugly and I have to look at it every time I come home."

"Shut up, O." Salma entered the family room, holding a plate with a slice of orange *meskouta* on it. She used her free hand to tuck her hair behind her ear. With her pale olive complexion, Salma was a younger clone of their late father and never ceased to give her fraternal twin brother a run for his money.

Yasmine chuckled because she was bad mouthing him, while eating the Moroccan traditional cake he'd baked earlier.

"Salma," Grandma Olly cautioned.

"Leave her, grandma. *Je sais où la chercher.*" Omar threatened. "In her stomach, right where it hurts." He picked up the remote to change the channel.

As everyone settled into idle chatter about their week and upcoming things they had planned, Yasmine couldn't help but shed a tear. They had come a long way from when their grandmother first came to the group home in Rabat to get them. Her mother, Bella DuBois, her grandmother's only child had eloped with a man her parents didn't approve of. The man – their father

– Ahmad Arazi, turned out to be what their grandparents predicted. A gold digger.

Yasmine and her siblings loved their father, but began to fear him when things changed in their family. When her grandparents cut their mother off and the money dried up, the beatings started. It all came to a head when the family was on their way home from a function.

"Yas, are you okay?" Mustafa asked with Anisa asleep on his shoulder.

She wiped the corner of her eye with her pinky finger and sniffled. Luckily, Salma and Omar were engrossed in the program they were watching, and their grandmother had dozed off. Mustafa stood and laid Anisa down on the sofa. Her big brother was their protector. At thirty-six, he was still single, but didn't lack female attention. He told them he wouldn't settle until he found a reason to. Straightening to his six feet two-inch frame, he flexed his broad shoulders and walked over to her. He stretched his hand and pulled her up.

"*tueal wamishi maei*. Come walk with me."

They made the short walk to the foyer and Mustafa leaned against the wall. The stare of his dark eyes was intense. He could read her better than anybody.

"Talk to me."

"I told you I was fine."

"We can stand here all day until we get an audience, or you tell me what's wrong so I can make it better," he said.

"You do know you can't fix everything."

"And you know you can't control everything. Especially your emotions which you try so hard to contain."

Yasmine shrugged. Raw emotion clogged her throat, so she didn't trust herself to speak.

"It's not your fault Yas. *laqad qult lak dhlk lisanawat.*" He pulled her to him, and she welcomed his burly arms around her. "I've told you that for years." She laid her head on her brother's chest for a few moments.

"I know it's silly, but I can't *not* think about it sometimes. Especially this year when Grandma Olly mentioned I'm depriving Anisa of security and stability."

When her brother didn't answer immediately, she raised her head. He was her number one supporter, but if he was silent maybe he thought so too.

Mustafa smiled, showing off his high dimples. "Stop looking at me with those eyes. Number one, it's not your fault. You'd just turned ten. You wanted something else for dinner as any ten-year-old sometimes does. That father got angry when mother asked him for money and pushed her wasn't your fault. Two, I'll always support what makes you comfortable. If you decide to spend Christmas with us here in Tweedes, fine. If not, do what you feel is best. We'll be here when you get back."

Yasmine looked at him and smiled. Although they'd never tell him, his approval meant the world to each one of them. Her brother's point of view was what she needed to make up her mind. She and her daughter would be on that flight to Kenya come December twentieth.

"I love you."

"And I love you back. Now let's go so you can take my niece home. Do you still leave for Botswana on Thursday?"

"Yeah and I'm taking Anisa with me. It's a quick trip. We'll be back Saturday afternoon."

Mustafa nodded.

Yasmine knew her grandmother would be disappointed she didn't heed her counsel, but she couldn't do it. She made a mental note to get with her deputy manager, Mr. Belkacem, again. She wanted to double check every aspect of the benefit to ensure its success. Her plan to leave Tweede Kans Cove before it took place on Christmas Eve was solidified.

*choo...*

"Excuse me."

Yasmine looked up from her phone and smiled at her daughter. She set the phone down and stretched out her arms. It was Saturday and they had landed in Marrakech from Gaborone, Botswana several hours ago. Now they were on the tail end of the three-hour ride to Tweede Kans Cove.

"Bless you. Come here, baby."

Anisa sniffled and moved closer to her with her tablet in tow. Yasmine lifted her into her lap.

"We'll soon be home, okay? And I'll make some of that chicken soup that you love."

"You won't put peas in it right?"

Yasmine rubbed her nose against her daughter's. "Do you like the way Uncle Omar makes it?"

Anise nodded and smiled, displaying the space that awaited a permanent tooth. "Yes, but he doesn't put peas."

*That's because he purees them, so you won't see them.*

"Of course, he doesn't. I'll make it like that and you'll drink some orange juice."

"Okay Mummy. How long before we get home?"

"About an hour more."

Satisfied, Anisa leaned back into her and swiped her thumb against her tablet's screen. The cartoon she was watching reappeared and once again she was lost in her own world. Yasmine pulled the blanket from the other side of the Range Rover Sport and covered them.

Leaning her head against the window, Yasmine shut her eyes and let out a labored breath. Exhaustion had crept in and her throat itched. She cleared it. Getting sick wasn't an option. She was determined to get home and combat the nuisance.

Seconds later, she opened her eyes and took in the stillness of the early December evening. As the car ate up the road, she admired the scenic mountain views. Snow accumulations in the nooks and crannies of the mountain were tell-tale signs of fresh snowfall. This was also about the time tourists and holiday vacationers flooded the small town. Grand Amour remained at capacity from the last week of November to the first week in January. Having travelled around the world for school and business, the fact that snow fell at all on the African continent still amazed her.

The town which had, as of last count, a population of a little over one hundred and twenty-eight thousand people, had been home to her for twenty-four years. She and her siblings were born in Fez. For a while, her parents moved from town to town. She never understood why. Just when she'd become familiar with a place, it would be time to leave again. Her father worked as a bellhop in a hotel while her mother stayed back home to take care of them.

As an adult, she now knew the reason they moved around so much was their grandparents would get a wind of where their daughter was and came looking. They wanted her back home. Just when they got close, her parents moved them. Yasmine dealt with it by not getting attached to anything.

If she had known that the next time they moved, she would be less two parents, she would've cherished those moves more. That fateful night when her father pushed her mother, she hit her head on the edge of the coffee table and never woke up. She slipped into a coma and later died. It was two days before Christmas.

*Christmas-1 Yasmine-0.*

Their father was arrested and went to prison and he also died some years later. They were moved to a group home where they stayed for a few months before their grandparents came to get them. Up until then, Yasmine and her siblings didn't know they were from Tweede Kans Cove. They didn't know their mother came from a wealthy background or anything about their grandparents.

That uneasy feeling that always came over her this time of the year returned. She hated letting her grandmother down, but her resolve from the last family brunch was solidified. She had to get out of Tweedes.

Three hours later, Yasmine leaned against the doorframe to Anisa's room. She was fast asleep. All that could be seen was a mass of brown curls peeking out from the Princess Zuri themed comforter. She was obsessed with the Marvel character. Yasmine tiptoed with caution, careful not to wake her, or step on any of the dolls she had on the floor. How she had the energy to play with them after their long trip, she had no idea. She picked up the dolls and the extra pillow which had somehow landed on the opposite side of the room. Placing the dolls in the bin and the pillow at the foot of the bed, she shook her head, sighting Anisa's dangling left leg. Yasmine tucked it back under the covers. Anisa stirred but didn't wake. She was a heavy sleeper and a wild one at that. As she did every night, Yasmine knelt by the head of her daughter's bed and prayed.

"Dear Lord, thank You for bringing us back home safely. Protect us through the night. Heal our bodies so we do not succumb to this cold. In Jesus Name. Amen."

She brushed her lips lightly against Anisa's forehead and exited the room. Yasmine walked through her home, ensuring all locks and windows were secured. At the back of the resort on the south side, she and her siblings each owned half an acre where their individual cottages sat. Each four-bedroom, three-bath, single level dwelling enjoyed a panoramic view of the mountain and ocean. They all had spacious living, dining, kitchen areas, a home office, covered porch and a spacious deck.

Yasmine decorated her space in black, burnt orange and beige colors. She walked into her kitchen, made a cup of lemon tea and headed to her room. Slipping into her bed, she picked up her phone to check her emails. The weekends were quiet, but she liked to be on top of things. For the next few minutes, she scrolled through social media. Not seeing anything worth spending time on, she put her phone away and picked up her Kindle. She stayed away from anything romantic. Action adventures, that was her thing. No use reading about something that had failed her on more than one occasion. Those stories were fairytales and she lived in the real world.

An hour and an empty cup later, Yasmine tied her silk scarf on her head and lay down with the aim of calling it a night. Seconds later, her phone chimed, and she felt around for it. Panic set in when she flipped the device over to read the subject line of an email from her deputy manager titled "Unforeseen Circumstances."

She quickly swiped the screen to read the full email that started with "I'm sorry." Her heart plummeted when she read that he had to be admitted to the hospital for pneumonia. She quickly responded, sending him her well wishes and made a promise to visit him during the coming week.

Yasmine lay back down and closed her eyes. It had been a long few days. She was grateful the next day was Sunday. She planned to do nothing. The thought of doing nothing and the email she'd just received made her eyes pop open. She hurled herself back into a sitting position as it dawned on her that Mr. Belkacem's assistant manager went out on maternity leave last month. That meant, she, Yasmine, would have to fill in. She picked up the pillow next to her, smothered her face with it and let out a gut-wrenching scream.

*This can't be happening.*

# CHAPTER 3

"Why can't we all go together? Like a family."

Kojo "Keyz" Sarbah felt the tension rise through his shoulders. The stress his son's mother and ex-wife had been giving him for the last ten minutes was slowly negating any work the masseuse he hired the previous day had done. He and the guys, the 891 Crew, had just gotten back from the European leg of their last tour. They had toured North America and at the beginning of the year, they would commence what they've dubbed the Selah Tour.

"Lydia, we're not a family. You and I made a wonderful human being and we raise him together."

"And whose fault is that?"

Kojo stopped cutting the tomatoes for his dinner and stared at his phone that was on the island. "Please, let's not do this again. We've been doing good." And they had. But it was something about this season that always had Lydia wanting to rehash their failed marriage which ended four years ago.

"Where are you taking him to anyway? Isn't he too young to be without his mother?"

Kojo resumed preparing the ingredients for a fried plantains and stewed gizzard dinner. It was supposed to be a lazy weekend for him, but turned out to be anything but. He had to go to his studio in downtown Accra and lay the beats for the soundtrack for some Christmas movie the guys had done. To get a vibe for the beat, he re-watched a rough cut of the movie titled *The Christmas Ultimatum* produced by KevStel Television.

That took longer than he expected, but he was just in time to make it to the Sarbah Soup Kitchen. It was an initiative he set up through his foundation a few years ago to feed the homeless. They had gone from feeding ten to fifteen people daily to averaging forty people. He was exhausted, but wanted a home-cooked meal. Now, all he wanted to do was enjoy his meal with some classic jazz Christmas music.

"Kojo, answer me. I hate when you wander off in your head," Lydia complained.

"What Lydia?"

"I asked where you're taking him."

"I haven't decided. Maybe the States or South Africa or maybe with the guys in Lagos. All I want to do is spend the Christmas holiday with my son. I've been gone for almost nine months."

"And Kwame misses you. This is why I told you to slow down," she nagged.

Kojo shook his head, telling himself it was time to end the call. If Lydia went down this rabbit hole, they would be there for the rest of the evening. He had to hear it when she was his wife. But that wasn't her role anymore. This was one, just one, of the reasons they couldn't stay married. She didn't understand or respect his passion and creativity and he, quite honestly, kept part of himself hidden. There was only one woman, well young girl, he had ever shared his heart with. Every other woman over the years got a piece of it. He wasn't fully committed emotionally to Lydia and shouldn't have taken it there. If it wasn't for Kwame, he wouldn't have.

"Okay Lydia, I'll call you later. This isn't about you and me. Kwame is five and I'm capable of taking care of him. I trust you'll do the right thing... for him." Kojo ended the call, not giving her the chance to respond.

An hour later, Vanessa William's *Star Bright* album played in the background while he stared at a muted movie on the television. His empty plate and glass were on a stool to the side. He looked around his fully decorated home. He'd hired a service to take care of the tree and Christmas décor while he was away. The seven-bedroom, six-bathroom home with a media room, man cave, small music studio and a state-of-the-art kitchen was his dream home. Built specifically to his taste. He had intended for a family to live there, but life didn't turn out that way. He and Lydia got a divorce before the home was completed. Now he longed for what he never had growing up. A family of his own.

*Father Lord, I'm ready. I want a family. I now know how to lead, love, protect and provide for them. I promise to make You proud.*

To the world, he was a rich, famous, award-winning music producer. The co-owner of New Sound Records, with sweet endorsement deals and an abundance of female attention. People thought his life couldn't be any better. But that was all a façade.

It had been two full years since he completed his intense therapy sessions. Even after he rededicated his life to Christ three years ago, he still needed to talk to someone. His childhood was marred with a whole lot of anger, self-worth issues and plenty of baggage he'd gladly carried along through adulthood. He wore the chip on his shoulder like a badge of honor.

Until that fateful night.

Kojo still talked to his therapist on occasion, but now he could manage better. That's why he knew he was now ready. Ready to open his heart and mind to what this season always had to offer – hope.

Recently, any time that word came to mind, he thought of one person. She was the one that made him even dare to believe it existed. But in return, he knew he'd hurt her. His phone chimed, breaking him from the memory that always ended in regret. He glanced at the caller ID. It was the band's former booking agent's assistant.

*I wonder what she wants.*

"Hey Tanya. Long time. Wassup?" he asked once he answered the call.

"Hey Keyz. I'm sorry to bother you but I can't get in contact with Yetty. I really need to talk to her."

Yetunde Phillips or Yetty, was the band's manager and there was no way he was giving her contact information away. "What's going on? What do you need? I can pass the message."

"Errmm, I need to talk to her about the band. My college friend's family needs a favor."

Kojo grunted. "Come on Tanya, you know we don't do favors. They don't pay any bills."

"Oh no, they'll pay. They're wealthy."

He decided to indulge her. "What's their name?"

"DuBois-Arazi."

Kojo's heart tightened. *Nah, there's no way. There's absolutely no way that God...*

"Hello?"

"Tanya, what's this friend's first name..."

"Salma...can you help me?"

"Give me her number," Kojo ordered.

As he ran to the kitchen for something to write with, he wondered, *God, are you for real right now?*

He wrote down the number while coaching his heart to slow down. First, he needed to know what Salma wanted. If it was what he thought it was, he'd still have the guys and Yetty to deal with.

# CHAPTER 4

*Ugh. Lord, help me get through this season.*

A week later, the song about decking the halls with holly blared from the town speakers as Yasmine made her way down Main Avenue. She'd just concluded a meeting at Beautiful Eyes and decided to walk the short distance back to her office. Top on the agenda was informing them that she was the new point of contact and providing an update on the event.

Despite all her efforts, she and Anisa did fall ill with the flu. They'd been stuck in their cottage for a week. What made it worse for her was that pulling off a successful benefit now fell in her lap. The realization that she would be spending Christmas in Tweede Kans Cove made her heart palpitate. Even though she'd had a week to coach herself into believing this year might be different, Yasmine could feel the tension running down her spine.

As promised, her deputy manager had someone send her an email on everything he had done and what was left to do. She'd had a couple of meetings from her bed, but now she was ready to get back to work. Yasmine might not be thrilled about Christmas, but she had a special relationship with Beautiful Eyes and her business and family's name was on the line. So, a successful benefit they would get.

"Merry Christmas, Yasmine," Mrs. St. Patrick, from the local bakery, yelled.

Yasmine lifted her hand, waved and returned the greeting. If she'd remembered she'd have to plaster on smiles as she wished the locals a Merry Christmas, she would've let her driver do the honors, while she hid behind the tinted windows. She pulled her wool cap down some to cover her ears; the cold was making her lobes numb. As she walked further down the street toward the Grand Amour Spa & Resorts, Yasmine lifted her cup of Nous-Nous coffee to her lips. She let out a soft moan. Ms. Bernadette strikes again. Among her special talents, the Beautiful Eyes Director also knew how to make one winning cup of Nous-Nous, with the perfect mix of hot milk over the pure black coffee.

Yasmine greeted more residents, trudging along with sparkling packages, evidence of early shopping. Joy, relaxed chatter and a festive spirit filled the air and she silently prayed again for help getting through the season.

"Yasmine! Yasmine...that special rug you ordered has arrived." Mr. Hassam yelled from the door of his Rug Designs Store, interrupting her thoughts.

"Hello Mr. Hassam, thank you. I'll be over later."

Yasmine passed by the Tweedes Museum and remembered the day she learned about the history of her town. The story went that in 1939, there was a servant in the King of Morocco's palace who fell in love with a French colonial master's daughter. It was a taboo at that time, especially since she converted him to Christianity. However, since he was one of the king's favorite servants, he wasn't killed, but banished from the area. The man and his new wife found this cove and settled here. The Christian community was built on a mix of Moroccan and French traditions. About ten percent of its population was made up of European expats.

As she turned onto Amour Lane and walked up the short stairs to the resort, Yasmine took in the fragrance of cranberries and cinnamon sticks, mixed with the smell of citrus and cloves.

She was far from a grinch, so her intent wasn't to steal the joy of the season from others. She just didn't want them suffocating her with it either.

❄

"Good news or bad news, which do you want to hear first?"

Hours later, Yasmine slowly lifted her eyes from the iPad in front of her and connected with her sister's. Questioning eyes stared back at her, as Salma waited for an answer. She was never one to hold any punches. She laid it bare and let the chips fall where they may.

"Why must they accompany each other? Why can't I just have good news? The past week has been rough. Have mercy on me, little sister," she pleaded.

A grin spread across Salma's face as she made it further into her office. "I'm sorry. I know you're just getting back to work. I saw you yesterday but still, how are you feeling? How is Anisa?"

Yasmine blew out a breath as she remembered the struggle to get her daughter out of bed this morning. She'd recovered, but still wanted to stay at home instead of going to the camp within the resort. Yasmine didn't have a nanny and needed to come into the office, so that wasn't an option. She hated to burden Grandma Olly.

Yasmine shrugged. "I'm good. As for her, health wise, great. But with you guys always giving her everything she asks for, she's borderline spoiled and that must stop,"

"Yas, lighten up, she's just a child. Since you're here, she must be in the activities' camp."

Yasmine ran her finger through her hair and nodded.

"Okay, I'll go check on her later."

Yasmine stretched her back. The smell of freshly baked bread and barbequed meat wafted into her office from the slight opening Salma created. Her stomach gurgled. Their offices were just above the resort's industrial kitchen.

"Omar must be cooking up a storm as usual and I'm ready for lunch. But first back to business, hit me. What's going on?"

As Salma was about to speak, her phone rang. She looked down at it. "Sis, I have to take this. It's the folks with the decorations. I'll be right back." She stood and exited while belting out instructions to the person on the other end of the line.

Yasmine pushed her chair back and a slight chill washed over her. Even after a second cup of cocoa, she was still paying for the walk she'd had in the brisk cold earlier. She strode over to her thermostat and adjusted it once again. She could still hear Salma's voice in the hallway. If anyone loved the holiday season, it was her sister. Part of her job was ensuring the guests enjoyed the feel, sights and sounds of any season they happened to be in during their stay.

The Grand Amour Resorts & Spa had fifty guest cottages, a fitness center and world class spa, three swimming pools, two restaurants, a golf course, tennis court and a boutique. While Tweede Kans Cove was the original location, they had two other running sites, in the eastern and southern parts of Africa. All of them were built the exact same way with the same level of exceptional service.

Mustafa always scouted the sites, closed the deals and along with their developer and architect, he oversaw the construction. Once that was completed, he came back home, and Yasmine would leave for the hiring process, training and ensuring operations ran smoothly. Omar took care of all the kitchen staff hiring and training while Salma ensured all guests got the same treatment, no matter the location. Managing all sites took them away from Tweede Kans Cove for several months at a time. Or longer when a new site opened.

The western location in Ghana was just completed and that would be her next stop come the new year.

"I love this time of the year, but my sanity is grateful it will all be over in exactly twenty days." Salma plopped down on the sofa in the corner of her office.

Yasmine chuckled at her sister. "New Year's Eve?"

Salma nodded. According to her, Christmas didn't end until the new year.

"That's because you love to do extra. And then the next year, you try to top the previous year's extraness. Grandma Olly says, 'Jesus is the reason for the season'."

Her sister's face contoured into a frown. "I do remember it's about Jesus. But there's also nothing wrong with wanting our guests to have a memorable time. You do know that people book a year in advance to spend Christmas here?"

How could she forget? It was the busiest time of the year for her. Because Tweede Kans Cove was the only one that boasted of snow, it was the most sought-after holiday destination.

"I get it."

"Come on sis, I know this time of the year is hard for you, but you said you'd try. I know this isn't what you had in mind."

"You're right." Yasmine saw the worry on her sister's face and decided she wouldn't rain on her parade.

"Are you sure you have bad news? It mustn't be that bad if it's taking so long to spit out."

Salma shifted to the other end of the sofa.

"What's wrong with you? Why are you moving?"

"If you swing, I'll be forced to swing back. And I don't want that. So, I'm making sure you can't reach me."

Yasmine laughed. Salma and Omar opted to go to college at NYU in the United States while she and Mustafa pursued their degrees in Europe. Their lingo was always so different.

"What have you done, Salma?"

"I don't particularly see it as bad news, who knows. But the way your French temper is set up, you might." Salma shrugged.

Yasmine stood. She was getting irritated at her sister's antics, and she was hungry. "I don't have time for this. The benefit is in two weeks. You remember? The one Grand Amour is hosting in conjunction with the church and I happen to now be at the front and center of it?"

"Uhmm. Yeah, this concerns that."

Yasmine's heart thumped. According to the update she gave earlier and her deputy's briefs, all the heavy lifting had been done. Food, games, items to be auctioned, the opening acts, even the headline musician... everything was in order.

"What's wrong? What happened? I was about to approve the wire for the balance of Adimu's fees to her manager, when you walked in the first time. What happened?"

"Sit down," Salma said. Her voice was now calm. "So last week when you were out, Adimu's manager called. She's not going to make it. There was a family tragedy and she couldn't handle the stress, so the doctor put her on strict rest until the new year."

"Oh my God. Did we send her flowers or something?"
Salma nodded.

Yasmine let out a sigh, then it hit her. Without Adimu, they wouldn't have any big-name musician. And without that, the probability of a successful event decreased. Beautiful Eyes was the biggest and only orphanage in the small town. Without enough funds, they would have to close their doors and move their residents to Ifrane. That wouldn't be good at all. Hence this benefit. Her family had given all they could by law, but it wasn't enough. So, they decided to bear the cost of a benefit.

Yasmine began to pace. "What am I going to do?"

Salma stood and approached her. Yasmine stopped and her sister took her hands and looked her in the eyes. "You're now the chief planner for this event, but this is the DuBois-Arazi name and Grand Amour's reputation on the line. Remember what Grandpa Marcelle taught us?"

Yasmine nodded. "We all have a responsibility to keep the family great. So, we stick together, because if one falls, we all fall," she murmured.

"That's right. So, I handled it. I, through my connections, booked the hottest neo-gospel band out there."

Yasmine smiled widely. "Why didn't you start with that? That's great Sally."

Her sister rolled her eyes. "Oh, please not the corny childhood nickname."

Yasmine brought her hand up. Salma moved back.

"I promise you Yas, if you tweak my nose, we're fighting."

"Okay, I'm sorry. I'm just so excited. Adimu cancelled but you were able to fix it on such short notice." She walked back behind her desk and slipped on her shoes. "Let's go to lunch. I love when Omar is home. He keeps the kitchen smelling good." Yasmine stood in front of the small mirror on her wall and fluffed her hair. Then she noticed her sister had a funny look on her face.

"Why are you looking at me like that? Bad news, Adimu cancelled. Good news, you got another band. What's their name?"

"The 891 Crew..."

"Oh wow, I heard a couple of their songs some years ago. Their newer stuff has a nice beat. I thought they were in Europe touring their last great tour?"

"Yes, they're on a break..."

Yasmine made it to her door, but Salma was still standing in place. Now she was worried. Something more was the matter. "Salma, you're scaring me. What's wrong?"

"Remember, I love you and I didn't know. But now that I do, I'm excited and expectant because I want you to be happy again."

"I am happy."

True, she had been in a depressive state for a whole year. But then she was thirty, had just lost her husband in an accident and had a toddler. The day after Christmas, her husband told her he had to run to the store. Her devastation knew no bounds when she received a phone call six hours later. There had been an accident. Pierre was found with a female companion, his car wrapped around a tree. What was she supposed to do?

*Christmas - 2, Yasmine - 0.*

"Okay, that's neither here nor there." She played with her iPad for a few seconds. "Remember you said they had a nice beat?"

Yasmine nodded.

"That's because he's their producer."

Yasmine frowned. "He, who?" She stared down at the iPad her sister turned toward her. Her heart tightened. Heat prickled her skin, perspiration trickled down her armpits. Those dark brown eyes stared back at her, threatening to unravel everything she had spent the last eighteen years wrapping up with intention. Well, eight years, but she was the only one who knew about that one time.

She looked back up at her sister. Her eyes danced around in apprehension and burned with rage she struggled to hide. Yasmine returned her gaze to the picture.

Kojo Mills.

He looked just as cocky and confident as he did when he was eighteen. That time he made her a promise and she believed he'd keep it. So, she kept hope alive like a sick puppy. Only for him to hurt her repeatedly.

"Is he coming with them?"

"Yes. He isn't just their producer. He also co-owns the indie record label the group is signed to." Salma paused.

Yasmine could feel her eyes on her but refused to meet them. She didn't have a response, so Salma continued. "When I first called my contact, and told her my plight, I only asked to speak to their manager. Imagine my surprise when Kojo called me the next day."

"Why does this article say Kojo Sarbah?" Yasmine asked, more to herself.

As expected, Salma shrugged.

"I'm sure Mustafa knows," Yasmine sneered.

"Sis, he may or may not. Point is the benefit, which is the day before Christmas, is saved. I'm sure the big bad sister I know can put away her ill... or giddy feelings aside for the residents of Beautiful Eyes," Salma said.

"I see what you're doing and you're right." She stomped to the door. "And let's get one thing straight, the feelings are neither ill nor giddy. I have no feelings at all for Mr. Mills or Sarbah... whatever he goes by now." She stalked out of the room.

"Got it! No feelings at all," her sister said.

"I heard that," Yasmine yelled as she jabbed the elevator button to take her to the ground floor where the restaurants were. As she rode down, she took in a deep breath and exhaled. She had to put herself back together or this holiday would be ruined for everyone. The door opened and she got out of the elevator bumping into a guest.

"Oh, I'm so sorry. Excuse me," Yasmine said. She was losing it already.

"No problem dear." The older woman said, continuing her way.

Yasmine looked back at the Tweede Kans Cove souvenir bag the woman was holding. Tweede Kans Cove: Where Second Chances Are Born.

That was the town's slogan. A smile reappeared on her face. She had nothing to worry about then. Pierre was her second chance and she didn't want a third.

# CHAPTER 5

With his feet propped up on his table, Kojo stared at his phone. He was in the New Sound Records offices located in downtown Accra. The building was comprised of executive offices on the upper level and a state-of-the-art production studio on the bottom level. In his office, he had an enclosed bedroom and bath because most times, he found himself working through the night. There was also a small cafeteria and listening booths.

He looked around his office. At thirty-six, he had been in the music business for over a decade and he'd done well for himself. The 891 Crew was the group he spent the most time with, but other artists came from all over Africa and Jamaica for him to lay beats for them. He was proclaimed a "Beast on the Keys," hence the name Keyz. The awards, fame and money were great, but his five-year-old son, Kwame, was his greatest accomplishment. But he wasn't complete, not yet.

The thought brought him back to the face on his phone. He looked at his watch, the guys' flight should be arriving from Lagos within the hour. He had gotten them accommodations in town, but as usual, Adeniyi Silva, the lead singer and his closest friend, would stay with him in his home. He was grateful for the down

hadn't changed was her fiery temper. He had to have all the answers to the questions he knew she'd have.

❄

Kojo shot a dark look at his friend, Adeniyi. The crew had flown in from Lagos the previous night. After a few meetings, they hung out for a bit before retiring for the day. Earlier, they went to church, had a private brunch and were now back at his place. The rest of the group were out on the town.

"Stop looking at me like that. I've known you for eight years and never once did you tell me that the woman who got away was *the* Yasmine DuBois-Arazi."

Kojo shrugged. "She's just Yas to me."

Adeniyi chuckled. "Well, from what you just told me, she's not anything to you."

"I'm going to pretend you didn't say that. But really, you know I don't talk about my personal life."

"Keyz man, you don't have a personal life. You have a son and an ex-wife," Niyi said.

Kojo stood and walked to the bar in his man cave. "Whatever, man. Set up the game."

"Yeah but we ain't playing 'til you give me something. You know the band loves you, but I had to grovel and beg for the guys to agree to go anywhere on Christmas. You know that's a set rule for us. No gigs. That's family and reflection time. Even Yetty wanted to bite my head off."

Kojo handed him the Malta Guinness and laughed. He remembered the phone call he had with Yetty. Since he had no siblings, Yetty and Niyi were the closest thing he had to family. He had cousins, but these two were like his annoying little brother and sister.

"Okay cry baby, you get two questions. Go."

Adeniyi rubbed his hands together. "First off, I'm not a cry baby. I'm trying to help your old behind, since I've never seen you this scared to meet a woman."

Kojo mushed his head. "I'm not scared, stupid. And you're not too far behind me in age."

"Yeah whatever. And my guy, I'm only thirty-two. Let's keep that in perspective."

"Keep talking and watch me change my mind."

"I'm no longer that boy you met in the Detroit club. Don't play with me." Adeniyi paused. "Okay, first question, how did you let her get away?"

Kojo lifted his drink to his lips and took a sip. He dangled it between his fingers and absently pulled on his beard with his free hand. "Simple, we were young. After we met, we were stuck to each other like glue. At first, I thought she just had a crush because I helped her. But as the years passed, we formed a close bond. I'm cool with her siblings, but she and I were the closest. The feelings just grew man, deep. Just as I turned eighteen, I professed my love for her, but I was damaged, man. I had no business loving anybody. But I loved her, and my mistake was that I told her and bailed. She was just sixteen.

"Long story short, you know the story of my mom. I had just started to look for my family. When I finally contacted my uncle, I didn't expect him to move that quickly. I thought by the time they came back from their holiday I'd still be in Tweedes. But I wasn't. My uncle came swooped me...and you know the rest."

"Wow," Adeniyi said after a couple of minutes. "I mean I've seen that kind of stuff in those corny romantic movies my mom and sister like to watch, but I never knew the stuff was real... young lost love."

"If you shed one tear over there, I'm kicking you out of my house," Kojo threatened him to lighten the atmosphere. The somber mood he was already in threatened to suffocate him. He hated talking about his mom. He had since asked Jesus to help him overcome, but it was still a topic he despised.

His life was like something straight out of the movies. A

teenage girl left her home in Ghana to visit her brother in the Moroccan University. Had a one-night stand. Got pregnant, and at the advice of her friends, instead of going back to Ghana, she told her parents she was going back to school in America. In reality, she went to Tweede Kans Cove, had the baby, and left the newborn baby boy in front of Beautiful Eyes with one name...Kojo.

"My next question, why did you let all this time pass?"

Kojo thought about it for a bit. There was nothing spectacular – anger at his life, anger at her for pushing their connection so hard, anger at her engagement, his bruised ego – but the buck did stop with him. "Life happened."

"Okay I see you shutting down again. Well, you have two days to figure it out before you see her." Adeniyi stood and headed for the stairs. "In the meantime, let me go text Yetty some stuff Adaeze needs to get for me. You didn't tell me there was skiing. Snow in Africa, this I gotta see."

"Adaeze will soon quit. The way you run that assistant of yours around. And where you going? We not playing?"

"Nope. That was just to get your secretive behind to talk," he called over his shoulder as he climbed the staircase. "Speaking of games, when are you picking up my nephew?"

Kojo rubbed his forehead. That was another part of his life he'd messed up. Although Lydia hadn't said no when he told her, he was sure she still thought there was a chance of her going with them. He picked up his phone. He might as well get this out of the way now.

Kojo sighed. "I don't know yet, but hopefully, he'll come along."

Adeniyi laughed. "I told you when you were proposing to that girl. Don't sigh now. Whatchu tell me that time...let me do me. Okay playa, do you, but I want to see my nephew."

Kojo shook his head. "Next time, check yourself into a hotel."

"Yeah, yeah...don't be a cry baby."

# CHAPTER 6

For the third day in a row, Yasmine's eyes flew open before the crack of dawn. And like every other day, she swallowed the disappointment that she'd be spending Christmas in Tweede Kans Cove. This time however, anxiety had become an added emotion.

Who was she kidding? She did have feelings for Kojo. After all these years, she hated she did. What they were exactly was still a mystery. Disappointment? Anger? Hate? Indifference? Whatever they were, she wasn't ready to confront them. What she did know was, it wasn't love. Despite that knowledge, she knew she was being a coward, but she just wasn't ready. Not with everything else going on. Why did everything have to be so hard during Christmas?

*Christmas-3: Yasmine-0*

She grunted, felt around for her phone and lifted it to her face. It wasn't even six a.m. yet. She closed her eyes, said her prayers and sat up straight. She flung her robe around her shoulders and stood. These days, she rolled out of bed more tired than when she got in the night before. She dragged herself to the kitchen and put on the kettle for her morning mint tea. Ten days. Ten days till the event and she could breathe easy.

Moments later, Yasmine took her first sip of the comforting beverage and looked around her living area, making a mental note to get decorations. She hadn't done that in a while. Her mind drifted back to Kojo. He and the band wouldn't be in town until two days before the benefit. That was her only silver-lining. The less time he was in town, the better. She'd even taken the necessary precautions to have someone on her staff handle their hospitality.

She probably was making much ado about nothing. After their encounter eight years ago, she'd erased Kojo from every part of her memory. Especially since that disastrous meeting had pushed her into marrying Pierre. It was for her sanity and the only way to give her marriage a fair shot.

Since Salma had mentioned Kojo, Yasmine had scoured the internet to see what she could find. He was divorced, had a child and was a superstar. So who was to say he'd even given her a second thought?

Yasmine shook off the wild thoughts and decided to get ready for her day. She had to stop over at the DuBois Manior to see her daughter, who begged to spend some days with Grandma Olly. But first, she needed to stop at Beautiful Eyes. Ms. Bernadette had summoned. And when she did, you answered.

*Y*asmine dropped her bag and ran to steady the ladder that was about to tip over.

"Oh my God! Easy. What are you doing up there?" She looked up into the eyes of a boy who couldn't be more than ten or eleven.

"Oh, Issa come down from there. I was on my way." Ms. Bernadette scurried towards them.

Issa pouted and made his way down the ladder. "I was just helping."

Yasmine looked up to read the banner he was trying to hang, and it said, "Luke Day 14." She wondered what that was about, but had since resolved not to get caught up in the hoopla of the season.

"And you did, but next time let an adult help you." Ms. Bernadette hugged him, and he turned to leave, but then turned around and smiled at Yasmine.

"Thank you, Miss."

Yasmine looked into his light brown eyes. "You're welcome." She walked back over to where she had dropped her things to retrieve them. "That is one courageous young boy."

"Yes, he is," the older woman responded with a chuckle. "He reminds me of a certain young man you used to be quite fond of back in the day."

Yasmine rubbed the back of her neck. In her teens, she'd spent a lot of time in this place. It was where Kojo lived. Beautiful Eyes took children in from birth up to the age of eighteen that have either been abandoned, voluntarily or involuntarily, or kids that had been removed from violent home situations. Adoption laws in Morocco were so strict that often, these children ended up living there from birth right up to eighteen.

Over the years, Beautiful Eyes had evolved to a welcoming abode that had everything a child could want. However, the more upgrades that were made, the more money that was required. Funding from the province of Fez had slowed down and they were now in jeopardy. It was now up to the town. And that responsibility fell on her and Grand Amour.

"Well, if history is to repeat itself, he'll turn out fine," Yasmine responded ignoring the "fond of" comment. "Where's everybody?"

"They're in the back, getting prepared for the lesson from Luke chapter 14."

"Okay, I came with the finalized program. All the vendors are set and know when they should arrive to set up."

"Thank you, Yasmine. When Mr. Belkacem called and said he'd be out of commission, I kind of lost hope that everything would go on."

"Why? This is a Grand Amour event and not Mr. Belkacem's."

Ms. Bernadette smiled, but didn't respond. She walked into her office and Yasmine followed, needing an answer.

"Sit down," Ms. Bernadette said. She strode to the small kitchenette to put on a kettle of water. "Mr. Belkacem didn't just take the benefit as a job, he had skin in it. It was personal to him. He believed in what he was doing. That gave me comfort that he'd do what it took to make it a success."

Yasmine turned in her seat. "Are you saying I'm not committed?"

"No, not at all. You're committed but to you, and I hope I'm not offending you..."

Yasmine shook her head, her lips unable to form the lie. *Of course, I'm offended.*

Over the last several days, she'd worked very hard to ensure everything went smoothly. So yes, she was insulted.

"With you, it's another win, just another project to check off. So, I was worried." The older woman peered at her from the top of the file she was going through, as though daring her to challenge her statement.

Yasmine didn't trust herself to speak. She wanted to tell the older woman straight off, but she wouldn't hear the last of it from Grandma Olly. However, just when she thought Ms. Bernadette was done, she opened her mouth again.

"Since you hate Christmas, I thought this was something you'd wanna rush through to get out of your way."

Yasmine raised her brow. "I don't have to care about Christmas to pull off a successful event."

"I know that now. Forgive my judgment. That's why I called you here today. To apologize." She shrugged. "It's just that the event is called Hope for the Holidays and I wondered how someone who is anti-Christmas and without hope can advocate for it."

*Anti-Christmas? That's a new one.*

Ms. Bernadette brought her a cup of cocoa which she seriously considered turning down. However, the marshmallows floating at the top called her name. She took the cup with a forced smile. "Anti-Christmas. You think I'm anti-Christmas?"

"Oh, not just me, but the whole town," she said, as though that made it better.

Yasmine's eyes widened. "The whole town?"

Ms. Bernadette shrugged again. "Well your house is never decorated on the outside and I'm sure the inside either. You're not around during the holidays and when we gather for the celebration of the Thirteen Desserts at your grandmother's home on Christmas day, you're the only one missing. But then right when the season is over, you're back in town."

Small towns. No one ever minded their business.

"Well, I can assure you I'm not anti-Christmas and I'll do everything in my power to make sure Hope for the Holidays is a success."

"I know that now, dear." Ms. Bernadette patted Yasmine's shoulder as a grin spread across her face.

Something about the grin was sinister and for Yasmine, that was her queue to leave. She finished off her cocoa and stood. She thanked the older woman who walked back behind her desk.

"Oh Yasmine, one more thing."

Yasmine raised her brow, waiting on the woman to speak. Her phone chimed with a text. Her assistant confirmed that the issue she went to Botswana to rectify has been resolved. She nodded her head and smiled, clicking on the email that was referenced and browsed through.

"So, is that a yes?"

She looked up at Ms. Bernadette and furrowed her brows. "Is what a yes?"

"That you'll take part in our 24 Days of Luke?"

"The thing the young man was hanging?"

"Yes. Mr. Belkacem's was going to take part in it as a show of solidarity, but now he can't." The woman's expression was blank. Well, almost.

Yasmine narrowed her eyes, detecting a challenge and a smile behind the older woman's almost blank expression. The way she saw it, she could say no outright and let the town keep thinking she was anti-Christmas. Or she could feign interest, find out what the heck was 24 Days of Luke, then say no. Or she could just say yes and get it over with, to shut everyone up.

Deep down, she knew her grandmother probably had a hand in this. She and Ms. Bernadette were close. Mr. Belkacem's illness gave them the perfect opportunity. Only common sense stopped her from thinking they might have had a hand in the timing of his illness.

Being one to never back away from a challenge, and despite the warning sirens going off in her head, she asked, "What is it about?"

Ms. Bernadette explained how, from the first day of December, leading up to Christmas morning, groups of two or three read a chapter and shared a lesson from the book of Luke. After this, they came up with creative ways to stir up and fill one another with hope for Christmas. As the woman's mouth moved, Yasmine conjured up the best way to tell her no. She had no group, her siblings were all busy and...and nothing, the answer was just no.

"That sounds so beautiful and thoughtful, however, I'm going to have to pass." Yasmine gave her a fake pout. "You see I don't have a group and with the—"

Ms. Bernadette waved her off. "Oh, don't worry about that. You only need two people and I found you a partner." She stood and walked toward her. "He should be here any minute."

"He? Oh, no Ms. Bernadette. I have a lot to do. Trust me, with my sister, I'm already stirred with enough hope for the whole town."

Ms. Bernadette held her hand and cupped her cheek with her

other hand. "That's great then, you can share it with others who have none."

"I still have to plan for the benefit..."

"Nonsense, you just said all the plans are done. And all we're doing now are last minute things. I'm sure all those people that work for you are more than capable."

*Wasn't this the same woman who just insinuated she didn't have skin in the event? Now she was telling her to delegate.*

"Ms. Bernadette, I really have to go now." Yasmine made another attempt to leave the woman's office. She had no idea how a quick stop turned into this. She should've just agreed to be anti-Christmas and gone her merry way.

The woman's shoulders slumped, and she lowered her gaze to the floor in defeat. Yasmine bit the inside of her cheek and massaged her temple. This is what she meant by people trying to suffocate her with Christmas. "Okay, I'll do it. Who is my partner?"

There was a knock on the door. Ms. Bernadette's face changed in a split second. Glee replaced the previous frown. The older woman rushed to the door. Yasmine raised her brows and then rolled her eyes. She just got suckered. She had to admit, the performance was perfectly scripted and executed.

"Oh, my I'm so happy to see you. Come in, come in."

The person on the other side of the door hadn't spoken, however Yasmine felt the atmosphere shift. The hair on the back of her neck stood causing her skin to prickle. *No, can't be.* She shook her head, lifted her phone and dialed.

"Sal, the band for the benefit...they don't arrive till next week, right? Two days before the benefit?" Yasmine asked her sister once she answered the phone.

"Yeah, that's correct not until the 22nd. Why wassup?"

"Nothing just wanted to be sure. I'll talk to you later."

"Yas, are you okay? You sound panicked."

"I'm fine. Love you." Yasmine didn't wait for a response before she hung up. Before her mind could wander to the other possibilities, Ms. Bernadette returned with non-other than Kojo Sarbah.

Her heart thumped. She stumbled backwards. His unexpected presence was a physical blow. Regaining her composure, her eyes narrowed, her glare shifting from him to Ms. Bernadette. Without uttering a word, she turned, picked up her things and walked around them and out the door.

*Yep, I should've proudly worn the title of anti-Christmas and left a long time ago.*

# CHAPTER 7

$\mathcal{Y}$asmine paled. The color literally drained from her face. In those few seconds, she'd exposed her vulnerability and given him hope. As she whizzed by, the familiar vanilla strawberrish fragrance of her hair gave Kojo a feeling of nostalgia. This wasn't at all how he'd planned it. When he made the decision to fly in a week ahead of the guys, his intention was to see Yasmine in private. He figured he might as well get whatever treatment she was going to dish out, out of the way before his crew arrived.

The only people that knew he came in the previous night was Mustafa and Omar and now of course Ms. Bernadette. And that's only because he called her when he woke up earlier. She practically begged him to come here this morning, and now he knew why. Kojo turned to Ms. Bernadette, who sported a sheepish grin on her face. If he knew she was trying to set him up, he wouldn't be here. He turned on his heels and ran outside. He got to the front door and perused the parking lot. Seeing Yasmine open her car door, he broke into a sprint.

"Yasmine!" His voice halted her steps, but she didn't turn around. He approached but hesitated to touch her. He remembered she packed a mean punch.

"Hey Yas." He inwardly groaned at the mediocre greeting. Everything he planned to say to her over the last couple of days got stuck in his throat.

"It's good to see you." He tried again.

Yasmine turned and scowled at him. Kojo could feel the heat burning through her eyes. If this were those cartoons he watched with Kwame, he'd be burnt to a crisp.

Her eyelids twitched, which was something that always happened when she was trying to control her anger. He used the silence to take her in. He had travelled far and wide, and she was still the most beautiful woman he'd ever met. A lot of that had to do with her inner self, although she was still drop dead gorgeous on the outside. Her wild brown curls rested on her shoulders and framed her delicate, olive toned, oval shaped face. Her lips were colored with a pinkish gloss. And her pink cashmere sweater rested perfectly on her black pants.

Yasmine cleared her throat, halting his gawk. She drew in a breath then exhaled. "Hello, Kojo." Her right cheek lifted in a forced smile.

"Shouldn't you be in there with your co-conspirator?"

"Look, I had noth—"

"It doesn't matter. I must go. I'm sure you know your way around Tweedes. When the rest of your crew gets here, we can have a meeting to get things set up for the benefit."

*I know she didn't just cut me off and dismiss me? Like she doesn't know who I am.*

True, they had a lot to talk about and he had a lot of begging to do, but he was still Kojo.

Kojo tugged on his beard, contemplating how to respond when her phone chimed. He watched as she pulled the device out and scrolled through, reading something. Without giving him another glance, she entered the car. Completely ignoring him. He reached out to grab the door before she shut it.

"Yas…"

Her glare went from his hand to his face. "Move."

He raised his hand in surrender and stepped back. She was about to blow.

She started the engine. "Oh, tell Ms. Bernadette I'm no longer interested in her Luke thing."

"What's that?" His brows furrowed.

"She can explain it to you," Yasmine said, then closed the door and backed out of the parking space.

Kojo shoved his hands into his pockets and watched until the car disappeared. Shaking his head, he walked back into the building.

Minutes later, Kojo was back in Ms. Bernadette's office. She gave him a remorseful glance and shook her head. "That child has been on the run for a number of years. I was hoping seeing you would help her slow down."

"She'll be fine. I'll see her later," he responded trying to soften the tightness in his tone. There wasn't any need to go into details. She'd done enough already. He should've known she wouldn't let it go as she continued.

"She's not the same young girl you once knew."

*Correction. She's not the woman I once knew.*

"Something in her has died." Ms. Bernadette stacked some papers and put them into the standing filing cabinet. "When you called to say that you'll be here for Christmas, I honestly prayed that you'll be able to help her find what she's looking for."

Kojo kept his expression blank. It was so good to see Ms. Bernadette again, but if she knew he was the least bit interested in this line of conversation, she'd keep going. He'd stayed with her for eighteen years and knew how she operated. Now wasn't the time.

He needed to leave and look for Yasmine. She, he also knew. She might have been thrown off guard earlier, but he was almost certain she was now strategizing on ways to avoid him.

Although he hadn't visited Tweede Kans Cove since he left eighteen years ago, he reconnected with Ms. Bernadette right after his divorce. He was bent on making amends and he decided to start with her. Beautiful Eyes held a lot of bad memories for him, but she was the one bright spot. She had cared for him just like a grandmother would. The woman never had any kids so she treated him like family.

And although he wanted to wipe the town of his abandonment out of his life story, he couldn't. The experiences he gathered from here contributed to making him who he was. The good, the bad and the ugly. His therapist helped him see that. Since then, he called Ms. Bernadette when he could and sent a monthly allowance to her personal account. Through his foundation, he also contributed to the home.

She let out a deep sigh that brought him back from his memories. Over the next hour, he and Ms. Bernadette caught up on the latest happenings in the town. After he relayed Yasmine's message, she explained what the Luke thing was. He took the 24 Days of Luke pamphlet with the instructions from her. She asked him to try to get Yasmine to partake in it. He promised he'd give it a shot.

A shot was all he could promise because, after what he experienced in the parking lot, convincing her of anything wasn't going to be easy. The dynamic between them wasn't that simple.

From Mustafa's reception of him the previous night, he was convinced nobody else knew about the London club incident of eight years ago. Nobody but the two of them knew of the potent attraction between them. And how he'd unintentionally humiliated her because of it. No one knew of the disaster his life became after that and the near-death experience it took to get back on track.

The issues between him and Yasmine were more than a childhood crush or a teenage love gone wrong. It was an adult blunder he wished he was man enough to fix then instead of allowing several years to pass by. In his defense, he was a broken man. A broken man who was toxic to every woman who tried to love him. Until he healed himself, he couldn't value her. How was he to love her when he hadn't even loved himself?

✳

"*H*as Yasmine been here?" Mustafa swirled around in his seat and gave Kojo a death stare. Kojo raised his hands in surrender. Ms. Bernadette kept him at Beautiful Eyes longer than he had expected. What started off as just an update on that Luke thing turned into a full-blown tour of the facility.

She was so endearing, meddlesome but still sweet. Every room they stopped by, she introduced him as her "grandson." No matter how many times he whispered he had to leave, she ignored him and kept going. After a while, he decided to let her do her thing. That decision, he now knew, was a big mistake. He'd been searching for Yasmine for over an hour and she was nowhere to be found.

*Where could she go in this small town?*

"You've been in town for barely twenty-four hours and you've run her away already?" Mustafa questioned, standing to his feet.

Kojo opened his mouth to speak but Mustafa cut him off. "What happened to laying low until we all had dinner later this evening?"

"That was the plan. But then I had to go see Ms. Bernadette. How was I to know Yasmine would be there?"

Mustafa laughed. "Oh, she was there? Our grandmother pretty much guilted her into handling the benefit program and to top it off, her deputy fell ill." He chuckled again. "Left to my sister, she would've been out of Tweedes by now."

"What happened man? The Yas I saw is different."

Mustafa shrugged. "She's older..."

Kojo scratched his neck. "No, it's not just that. I mean, she's still fine. Sexy, beautiful, in fact, gorgeous—"

"Enough, I get it, move on."

Kojo laughed at him. Mustafa was protective, but he wasn't one of those brothers under the illusion that their sisters couldn't date. When they were younger, he never gave him a hard time about he and Yasmine hanging out.

"I know she probably can't stand me, but it's something else. And what's this about her leaving during Christmas?"

Mustafa shut down his laptop and picked up his keys. "That my friend, is her story to tell. That's if you can get her to talk to you."

Kojo groaned. "You know that sister of yours keeps a mean grudge."

"*Vrai*. True. But I'm sure you knew what you were up against. So, while you try to get a little cheer in your holiday, I'm going to town hall for a meeting with the Mayor."

Kojo followed him out. "I'm headed to the Manior to see Grandma Olly. I know I'm gonna get a mouthful."

"Oh definitely. You have like an eighteen-year arrears."

"You're not funny."

"I wasn't trying to be. Even I couldn't get a phone call from you until you called to ask about Yasmine's engagement, and I had to threaten you to stay in touch."

"You didn't scare me – you know that. But I get it, the memories hurt but not all of them, so I should've..." Kojo let his statement trail off. He owed Yasmine an explanation before anybody else.

"I called over there. Grandma Olly is back. The housekeeper also said Kwame is doing good. I still can't believe you have a son."

"Yeah, some days I can't believe it myself." They walked out of the resort. A cool breeze accompanied with sunshine enveloped him. Kojo loved this weather; that was among the things he missed about Tweede Kans Cove. He took in a breath and allowed the clean scent of the ocean's breeze to waft through his nostrils. He and Mustafa dapped with a promise to see each other later.

"Aye," Kojo called out, causing Mustafa to turn. "If you see your sister before I do, just text me."

"Only if she doesn't kill me first."

Kojo smiled as Mustafa entered the back of his car. He watched until the driver pulled off. He made a mental note to check on his friend later. Yasmine just might kill him.

He chuckled, pulled up his collar, stuffed his hands in his jeans pockets and headed to face another woman he knew he'd pissed off – Grandma Olly.

# CHAPTER 8

*I*t was just like any regular night. A time when she was carefree. She had just turned twenty-six years old and a group of her friends had decided to go to a London club. There were drinks, food, wonderful music and great conversation. She had since gotten over the hurt of Kojo leaving Tweede Kans Cove. She had since gotten over the pain of his rejection when she reached out to him once she started college several years ago. He told her what they had was puppy love and she should get over it. As though that wasn't enough humiliation for her, she tried to be his friend when she was about to enter graduate school. That time he had someone who said she was his manager tell her to leave him alone. Calling her a distraction.

Yasmine resolved to live her life and she was enjoying every bit of it. She was glad to, for the time being, get out of Tweedes and away from her grandmother's constant questioning about when she would settle down. All she wanted to do was enjoy the summer. But then, he, Kojo Mills, got on stage. Imagine that, he walked into the same club. The first note he hit sapped all the joy out of her carefree night in London right out.

Kojo had just finished performing a set and the crowd went wild with applause. The grin on her face made her cheeks hurt. He *was a jerk, but she was proud of him. Despite all the time with no communication, Yasmine kept up with his career. That was the first time she had seen him perform. The first time she'd seen him physically since he left Tweede Kans Cove. He wasn't famous, but he was gaining a heavy audience on the internet. And at that moment, she understood why.*

*Her friends wanted to go backstage to get his autograph. Ever since she was called a distraction, she hadn't spoken to him, so she hesitated. After being called moody and a spoil sport, and any other adjective that insinuated she was bringing the party down, Yasmine agreed.*

*"Since when do you go to clubs?" Those were the first words out of Kojo's mouth when her girls left them alone in his dressing room. They had all fawned over him and he signed autographs and took pictures with them.*

*"Don't act like you know much about me Kojo." Yasmine rolled her eyes.*

*"Yeah, you're right. I don't. Is the whole family here with you in London?"*

*"No, I'm here by myself. Just for the summer, then it's back home."*

*The conversation and static between them was awkward. Her eyes left his and travelled around the room, not really looking for anything. She shifted her weight from one foot to the other. This man who stood before her was a far cry from the boy who teased her, comforted her, fought her battles, was her best friend, and first love. This person was a stranger, one who kept himself closed off to even her. She should have listened to him when he told her some years ago that what they had was nothing. The love. The friendship. It was all nothing.*

*"I should get going." She turned toward the door.*

*Kojo stood and walked closer to her. He held her hand to stop it from fidgeting. Then he walked her backwards until she was against the wall. She could feel the vibrations from the music in the club through the thin wooden wall. It matched perfectly with the thumping of her heart. Her breath was coming in gasps.*

*"What are you doing, Kojo?"*

*He kept his eyes locked with hers but didn't answer her question. She couldn't deny the attraction, but there was something distant in his eyes and she wanted no parts of the Kojo she was seeing. Suddenly his lips came down on hers. The kiss wasn't gentle, it was rough. As though he was punishing her for something she didn't even know she'd done. His hands began to travel up her legs, panic took over her senses and with all her strength she pushed him back.*

*"What are you doing?"*

*"Isn't that what you wanted since you can't seem to stop following me around?"*

*"Following you? I didn't even know you'd be here."*

*He shrugged, licking his lips. "Why can't you remain in the past where I left you Yasmine?"*

*Her brows arched in disbelief. "What happened to you?"*

*Ten years had gone by and people do change, but she couldn't reconcile who she grew up with and this person who stood in front of her.*

*"Nothing happened to me, but apparently you want me to happen to you."*

*"Huh? The last time I talked to you was when I was about to start college. The last time I tried to reach out, you weren't man enough to call me a distraction yourself." Her voice shook. "You know what? Doesn't even matter, I could care less what happened to you." She stomped over to the door and turned the knob when she heard her name.*

*"Yas—"*

*There was pain in his voice, but she couldn't do anything about it. She had tried to remain his friend over the years but got shot down every time. She had never done anything to him.*

*"Goodbye, Kojo. Have a nice life."*

*He had taken her evening and turned it to crap. But it was nobody's fault but her own.*

"Ms. Yasmine, do you want me to warm that up for you?"

The sound of Ashley's voice brought her back from the past. Yasmine felt her cup of now cold cocoa. She glanced up at the high schooler who worked at the Sip & Relax Café with her parents when school was out.

"Erm, no. Could you bring me some mint tea instead?"

"Sure." She turned to leave, then paused. "It's going to be okay, Ms. Yasmine."

"Excuse me?"

The teenager shrugged. "I just thought to tell you that. You seem very sad. My grandma says Christmas is the season to rejoice in victory. Because the devil couldn't stop Jesus from coming to earth to die and resurrect for us." She bent as though she was about to tell a secret. "So, whatever is making you sad, rejoice that you have the victory over it too."

Yasmine's eyes followed the teenager who walked away without waiting for a response. It was a good thing since she didn't have one.

For the first time since she had been there, she took in the Café. The tree was up, festive music played in the background and the place was decorated in the traditional green, red and white colors with Moroccan Christmas lamps hanging over each table. The aroma of fresh pastries and brew added to the warmth that was a huge contrast to the cool atmosphere outside.

Yasmine's eyes darted to the clock on the wall and she rested her forehead in her hands. If it was correct, that meant she'd been there for three hours. She had things to do. Ducking and dodging Kojo wasn't one of them.

She raised the *cornes de gazelle* to her mouth, groaned and took a bite. Yasmine had rehearsed in her head several times how she'd react when she saw Kojo again. All of it went out the window once her eyes locked with his. In her mind, he'd be here with his friends two days before the benefit. She had planned out her agenda for those few days where she might not have to see him at all. Now he was here a week early and without his friends. How was she supposed to duck and dodge him for a whole week, without looking bothered?

"Grandma Olly, I apologize again for staying away for so long. It's what I thought I needed at the time."

"Stop apologizing to me, son. You've been doing that for the past hour," her grandmother responded. "I understand your explanation. What I want you to understand and I think you already do, is everything you go through in life happens for a reason. No experience is just because. It's left for you to learn from it and move on to better, or dwell in it and be stuck in a rut." She paused. "*Tu comprends?*"

"*Oui je comprends*. I understand."

Leaned against the doorway, Yasmine rolled her eyes as she listened to her grandmother and Kojo's conversation. She'd forgotten he spoke French too. She was about to make her presence known when Anisa came barreling into her.

"Hi, Mommy." Anisa's hands went around Yasmine's waist in a tight hug.

"Hello, my angel. Were you a good girl for Grandma Olly?" Yasmine bent to kiss her on her forehead.

"Yeah, I was. Oooh, I have a new friend. Hold on Mommyyyyyyy." She ran down the hall and seconds later a small boy with dark chocolate skin, brown eyes and a Mohawk haircut accompanied her daughter. Before she could speak, Kojo and Grandma Olly came around the corner. Her eyes moved from the boy to Kojo. The resemblance was striking.

*So, this is his son?* She wondered if the boy's mother was with them here in Tweedes. The realization that she had an audience forced a smile on her face. She walked over to her grandmother and kissed her cheek.

"Hi Grandma, hope Anisa didn't give you too much trouble?"

Her grandmother waved her off. "No, she was fine." The older woman looked from her to Kojo. "I'm assuming both of you met earlier?"

Yasmine glared at his nervous eyes.

"Hey, Yas," he spoke.

"Yes, I saw him earlier today at Beautiful Eyes." She looked down at the boy. "And what's your name handsome?"

"Kwame," the boy responded.

Yasmine smiled and stretched out her hand. "It's nice to meet you, Kwame."

The little boy shook her hand, right as Grandma Olly announced she was going to rest her head.

*Yeah right. I know what she's trying to do and it's not happening. They are her guests.*

The minute she heard her grandmother's bedroom door close, she motioned Anisa to get her coat. Kwame followed her. Yasmine could feel Kojo's eyes on her, but she refused to acknowledge him.

"Yasmine, can we talk?" he asked, his tone low.

She didn't even have to think about it. "No. Why are you here early? The contract with your band states you have to be here only two days before the event." She folded her arms across her chest. "Why are you here?"

He lifted his hand to his forehead and rubbed on it. "This is home."

"*Vraiment? Depuis quand?* Never mind don't answer that." She shook her head at him. "But just so we are clear, this benefit means a lot to my grandmother, and therefore to me. I'm not interested in revisiting the past. All I want for Christmas is for you to play the keyboard and leave town. That's what you do for the band right? So, do that and be on your merry way." She seethed.

The look in his eyes, she couldn't quite call. But then she didn't care to. He opened his mouth to speak when Anisa and Kwame approached.

"Are you ready?" Yasmine asked her daughter. "It was nice

meeting you, Kwame." The boy gave her a shy nod before walking over to his father and putting his hand in Kojo's.

"Yes, mommy. Bye, Kwame. Bye, Kwame's daddy."

Kojo smiled at her. "See you later, Anisa, and it was nice meeting you."

Without another word Yasmine turned to leave. As she got to the front door, she heard Kojo say, "We're not done, Yas."

"Yes, we are."

Yasmine grappled to control her temper as she snapped on Anisa's seatbelt. Christmas never failed her. Once again, a bad memory was around to dampen her already struggling spirit.

*Christmas-4: Yasmine-0.*

# CHAPTER 9

The next day, Kojo woke up early, because once again, he couldn't get his mind to be still. He'd tossed and turned all night. Going over the what ifs, what nows, and calling on hope. He rolled out of bed in his pajama bottoms and opened the curtains to another Tweede Kans Cove morning. The sun was just peeking over the horizon and the skyline looked like the cover of a postcard.

He opened the balcony door connected to the guest bedroom Mustafa assigned to him, and the clear ocean breeze hit him. He inhaled deeply and exhaled, rotating his shoulders to loosen up. The miracle of creation settled in his soul. The thought led him to the hope Jesus provided when He came on the scene. The sick being healed, blind given sight, crippled made to walk, the hungry, fed. His lips turned up in a smile. The supernatural power of God takes no breaks. He was going to speak and expect his miracle; this was the Christmas season after all.

"God of creation. Give me the words to say. Soften her heart to listen. I really messed up, I know. I couldn't do anything about it then. I can now. Help me. In Jesus name. Amen."

He walked back into the room. It would be another hour before Kwame woke up, so he decided to change into some warmer clothes and go for a walk along the coastline. Several minutes later, with "Little Drummer Boy" by the Kenyan Boys Choir playing through his ear buds, Kojo took brisk strides along the shore. There were a few early morning dog-walkers in the distance.

There was one walker whose walk he could never mistake. He stopped in his tracks and observed Yasmine. Her hands were shoved into the pockets of the yellow hoodie she wore over some black jogging pants. The pants clung to her hips and he had to force his eyes to look the other way. Her dark brown hair was in a bun, but the ocean breeze had most of it flying all over her head. Her pace wasn't as fast as someone exercising, more like someone in deep thought.

Kojo continued on to her. As though she could feel a presence behind her, she looked over her shoulder. Catching a glimpse of him, she stopped. Her eyes widened with surprise and then rolled with annoyance.

"Morning, Yas," he said. He knew he sounded so lame. His boys would clown him if they saw him now. "How are you?"

She glanced at him, then turned to walk away. "What do you want Kojo?"

"Can't I just want to say good morning and ask how you are?"

She shook her head and took ear buds out of her pocket and stuffed them in her ears.

Kojo chuckled. She had always been petty. "That's childish Yas. Come on. We can at least be civil."

She continued to walk away, not answering him. He glanced up to the sky, whispered a plea for help and jogged up to her. He reached out to touch her arm which halted her steps. Her eyes narrowed and a crease graced her forehead. Nothing she did would scare him off as he deserved it all.

"Okay, you have my attention. What?"

"I'm sorry."

"Okay." She turned.

He grabbed her arm. "It's me KJ," he pleaded, using the nickname she had given him when they were teenagers.

"No, you're not. What's it they call you now?" She placed her index finger over her lips, then snapped her fingers. "Oh yes, Keyz."

"I deserve that. All I ask for is one dinner."

"No." She shook her head.

"Coffee? Tea? Fekkas? A sandwich?" He continued to run down the options, but she shook her head at each one. "Yas, come on. It's Christmas, the season of giving. Just give me your time for conversation. I can explain and I deeply apologize."

She laughed. "Didn't they tell you I don't do Christmas?"

"You what? Since when? You would get a little sad the day before Christmas, but you always enjoyed the season." He knew something about her was different, but this was ridiculous. Didn't she see what a wonderful gift God gave them with the birth of Christ?

"Kojo—"

"KJ," he corrected her.

"*Hein*? I'm not calling you that—"

"Why? Brings back too many memories?" he teased.

She folded her arms across her chest. He must have struck a nerve because that was her defense stance. In that moment, he knew that this wasn't the way to get to her. He was going to have to force her to listen to him. Yasmine had always been stubborn and resilient. Once she took a stand that was it. He was going to get nowhere with her pleading and begging. He'd do that for her any day, but now he needed her to hear him out.

He walked closer to her invading her personal space. He heard her breath hitch. He smiled inwardly. His heart thumped and he could hear hers do the same. His six foot frame towered over her five feet six or seven inches. No matter how much time went by, the attraction between them was never in question.

He stared down at her. "Yasmine DuBois-Arazi, let me reintroduce you to Kojo Sarbah. Nothing's changed baby, except age. Don't make me kidnap you just to talk to you."

"That's where you're wrong. A lot has changed. Chief among them is I no longer care about what you have to say."

He lowered his head, his lips slightly above hers. He could feel her shiver. "Are you sure about that?"

"Y...es..." she stuttered.

"Or are you scared of me?" he asked, and her eyes narrowed. *I got you baby*. One thing with Yasmine was that she never backed down from a challenge.

"You want a sit down? You want to talk? You have things you need to say? Okay, meet me at my cottage in two hours," she said, with a smirk.

That was too easy. What did she have up her sleeve? "What's going on Yas?"

She shrugged. "You were the one that wanted to talk. I'm giving you a chance to." She turned and walked away.

"Yas! Yasmine," he called to her.

"What? Are you scared of me? Meet me at my cottage in two hours," she threw over her shoulders and walked away.

*H*e had underestimated her. Big mistake. Now he was at Tweedes Memorial Hospital reading to a group of sick children. He had no problem with doing it, but when he asked to sit down and talk, this wasn't what he had in mind.

Kojo had met her at her cottage with Kwame in tow. He thought he would let Kwame and Anisa play while they talked. No such luck. Instead, she served Kwame and Anisa a warm breakfast of eggs, sausages and waffles. With juice and cocoa to wash it all down. She was so petty that she didn't even offer him anything until he asked. She then pointed him to some croissants and whipped cream and the coffee pot.

When they were younger, he would've put her in a chokehold. But now, he was at her mercy. His eyes darted toward her talking to the Director of the hospital. They were a little too friendly for his liking. The man had spent the whole time whispering in her ear, under the guise Kojo presumed, of not wanting to make noise.

"And that's the true meaning of Christmas," Kojo said, closing the book he was holding.

"I like the story, but I'm sad," one of the kids said.

"Why?" Kojo asked. The boy had tubes in his nose that were attached to the oxygen tank hooked to his wheelchair.

"Because I thought it was about presents."

Kojo chuckled. "Yes, you can get gifts that day, but remember it's best to give to those in need. Jesus was born because God knew we needed Him if we had any chance of getting into heaven. So even though you get physical presents, the gift God gave us in Jesus is the best gift of all."

The boy nodded. There were a few murmurs between the kids before the head of the children's wing came in and gave another speech, ending the occasion. Kojo stood and it was only when the kids clapped that Yasmine drew her attention away from the Director. Kojo clenched his jaw. It was lunch time and Kwame and Anisa were in the resort activities center. Yasmine had had her little fun, now he was going to have his sit down.

"That was very funny, Yas," he said as they stepped out of the hospital.

"I have no idea what you're talking about. You wanted to sit down and talk. I made that happen. You should be thanking me." She glanced at him before turning her attention back to her phone. "Or celebrities don't talk to sick kids?"

"You know I have no problem talking to them. But that wasn't what I meant when I asked for a sit down."

They were now seated in the back of her town car as the driver drove them back to the resort.

"It wasn't?" she feigned surprise.

"You know it wasn't."

Kojo started to speak again when her phone rang. She answered and based on her side of the conversation, the delivery of the auction items for the benefit was being delayed.

"No, I can't wait till next week. That's the week of the benefit. I want everything in Tweedes before then." She ran her burgundy painted nails through her hair. She listened a few more moments, then let out a deep sigh. "Okay, I'll have to send someone to Ifrane." She hung up the phone.

"I didn't sign up for all this," she murmured.

He was sure she thought it was to herself, but he'd heard her.

"What's going on?"

She looked at him. Her hesitation couldn't be disguised. She looked at her watch and sighed. "I'm going to have to make a trip to Ifrane."

"For the auction items?"

She frowned at him. "Yes, nosey. You do know that's rude."

"What? You wanted me to turn my hearing off?" He chuckled. "But anyway, why do you have to go?"

"Because they have to be inspected and since I'm stuck with the benefit and the other two people I can send are out of commission, I have to do it."

It was his turn to frown at her. "Stuck? I thought you liked Beautiful Eyes. What's going on, Yasmine?"

She turned away from him. He hoped she took his question as one of concern and not intrusion. They remained silent for a few more minutes. She looked at him. In that moment, he saw his friend, his love. The one he had pushed away because he couldn't handle his own demons. She opened her mouth to speak and, in a split second, raised his hope. Only to dash it the next when he saw her physically clamp up.

"Never mind. Where am I dropping you? I have to go." Her tone was laced with irritation.

"Isn't Ifrane about three hours away?" he asked, ignoring her question.

"Yes, it's noon. If I leave now, I'll make it back by nightfall.

But I have to get some things in order, so probably won't leave until one." All the while she was talking, she was sending a text.

"I can't allow you go by yourself."

That caught her attention. She paused and whipped her head towards him. "Allow? Kojo, please, I'm not in the mood. I've already asked Omar to go with me. What's this fascination with me? If I recall correctly, you wanted me to stay in the past. Now you're trying to insert yourself into my present," she said.

"Look, Yasmine. There's a lot you don't understand and I'm trying to right my wrongs. Why won't you just let me do that? A simple conversation?"

"Like I tried to talk to you all those times?" She let out a labored breath. "You said you're sorry. I said okay. What else is there?"

"Yas—'

"No, stop. What am I supposed to be? Your Christmas project? Am I your charitable deed? I'm good, Kojo. I did exactly what you asked me to do. Stay out of your way. Now stay out of mine."

After her rant, he let her be. He deserved her anger; he had been a real jerk to her. But he had his reasons. No excuses, but reasons. He pulled out his phone and sent Omar a text. He needed a favor.

# CHAPTER 10

Murder. That's exactly what Yasmine had in mind. How all her siblings turned to traitors just because Kojo showed up was beyond her. First, Mustafa knew he was coming to Tweede Kans Cove early and didn't tell her. Even offered him lodging. Now Omar, who had agreed to accompany her to Ifrane, left her hanging. At the last minute, something came up at the resort that he couldn't get anybody else to handle. They must really think she was stupid. The only person that seemed to be on her side was Salma. But she and Omar were twins and never kept secrets, so she could've been in cahoots with him.

Yasmin glanced to her side and rolled her eyes. The minute Kojo got in the car instead of Omar, she told him not to say a word to her. He chuckled, but did as she asked. Pissed was an understatement and the feeling hadn't dissipated in the two hours they'd been on the road. She shifted in the back of the town car again, let out a sigh and adjusted her ear buds.

"You still huffing and puffing?"

Her music had since stopped playing and she could hear him, but refused to dignify him with a response. She knew she was being unreasonable, but she was so fed up that she didn't even care. This wasn't how she envisioned this season would go at all.

She had accepted the fact that it had turned out this way, but why did other things have to keep coming up, making the already unpleasant situation more uncomfortable?

"You know sooner or later, you're going to have to talk to me. And a lot has changed but let me remind you that me getting what I want hasn't," he said.

Kojo didn't have to remind her of anything. She knew that all too well. That was the reason she wasn't open to listening to anything he had to say. The minute she did, she would be sucked up into him again. They had two separate lives. There was so much she wanted to know about his but dared not ask. The less she knew the better. Nine more days and this would all be over.

"I don't have to do anything. You've bulldozed your way on this trip. But you can't force me to talk to you."

He sighed and she hid her face with her hand. She didn't want Kojo to see her flushed cheeks. Any time she was in his presence, she had to will herself not to shiver from the looks he gave her. How could she still be attracted to him? She wanted to hate him.

Last night, she had another dream about his dark chocolate skin and physique that made it clear he missed no gym days. He'd let his black hair grow out and it connected to his perfectly trimmed beard. His full lips and dark brown eyes constantly invaded her thoughts. She hadn't thought through inviting him to her cottage, because now the enticing spicy, woody scent of his cologne wouldn't leave.

He closed the laptop that was on his lap. "Okay, how about you don't talk, but listen."

Yasmine turned to him in contemplation. The persistence in his tone and her memory of him confirmed what she had been trying to deny. He would pester her until she listened. Maybe if she did listen, and he got whatever it was off his chest, he would be out of her face and all these feelings she'd been trying to suppress since she saw him at Beautiful Eyes would go away.

"Fine, Kojo. One talk and you'll leave me alone?" she bargained.

"No, one talk over food. After that, if you want me to leave you alone, I'll seriously consider it," he countered.

"You're in no position to make a counteroffer," she said.

He shrugged. "I'm starving, woman. What I have to say would definitely knock the wind out of me if I did it on an empty stomach." He rubbed his stomach and creased his forehead as though it hurt.

"You do know with a son, you should really act your age."

"Says the woman who tossed stale croissants at me and told me to fetch my own coffee. While her and the kids ate a warm breakfast."

As annoyed as she was, she couldn't suppress her smile. Yasmine still couldn't believe she did that.

"So, blame yourself that I'm this hungry," he complained.

"I didn't tell you to come to my house without eating, and—"

He waved her off. "Yas, whatever. So, do we have a deal?"

She squinted her eyes at him, wondering what he had up his sleeves and if it was really going to be that simple. "Kojo..."

"Please don't tell me that the no-nonsense, fiery tempered, confident Yasmine DuBois- Arazi is scared to talk to me over food." He raised his brow in a challenge.

"I'm not scared."

Kojo made the sound of a chicken clucking. She narrowed her eyes at him and shook her head. "Fine. You talk, I listen, over food."

A smile spread across his face and he opened his mouth to speak, but she raised her hand to him. "Oh, let me clarify, this isn't a fancy dinner or a date. Just food."

"Okay."

Yasmine's frown earned her a wink from him and he opened his laptop back up and continued with what he was doing. That was too easy. She looked around. They were in a moving car, so she had no idea what she was looking for, but his simple okay made her nervous.

"You okay over there?" He smirked.

A smile danced around his eyes and she wanted to punch him. "Kojo, I'm serious," she warned.

"And I said okay."

Yasmine glowered at him for a few seconds. An eerie feeling came upon her. Had she just set herself up? She knew Kojo, or the former Kojo. Nothing was ever a simple okay.

"Ms. Yasmine. We're here," her driver's voice interrupted the silence.

Kojo got out of the car before she could ask him to wait for her.

"Okay good. I don't think we'll be long." She looked at the time on her phone. "We should make it back to Tweedes before nightfall." Yasmine put the strap of her bag over her shoulder and gathered up the folder that contained the list of items. Her door opened and Kojo held out his hand. She hesitated and looked at him.

"Come on, Yas. We need to get back, remember?"

Yasmine took his hand and he helped her out. Once he shut the door, a few flakes of snow fell on her head.

"There was no forecast of snow this morning," she murmured to herself.

They dashed into the building and she went straight to the receptionist, while Kojo stood at the corner on his phone. "I'm here to see Mr. Battuta. It's about my shipment of ancient artefacts and artwork for the Hope for the Holidays auction in Tweede Kans Cove. It should be under Grand Amour."

The woman nodded, dialed a number and politely told her she'd be taken to the back shortly.

With a terry robe secured around her, Yasmine dried her hair with a towel. This just wasn't her day. She thought "shortly" was ten to fifteen minutes max. That was the world's definition, she was sure. How it turned into an hour wait still infuriated her. The hour in the office then turned into another two-hour delay at the warehouse. Before everything was loaded in her truck, Mother Nature decided to laugh in her face. She was trapped in Ifrane until morning. If she knew it would snow, she would've stayed in Tweede Kans Cove. However, she didn't, because when she checked the weather before leaving, the app was on Tweedes' location and not Ifrane.

Yasmine tossed the towel in the hamper and lotioned her body. Her phone rang and she put it on speaker.

"Hey, Salma," Yasmine muttered under her breath.

"*la tahzan*. Don't be sad," her sister said. "It's just overnight. You know what the weather's like at this time of the year. Very unpredictable. It'll clear up."

Yasmine sighed. "Okay, I guess. *kayf hal tifli?*"

"Anisa is fine. She's asleep."

"Ugh." Yasmine regretted not calling earlier.

Salma chuckled. "You seriously need to see someone about your control issues. You can't control everything, Sissy. Sometimes you have to roll with the flow. Everything will work out."

"I hate leaving things to chance. Things never turn out right..."

"But you can't keep living like that. It must be exhausting, and I know you aren't happy. *'ayn tuqimin allayl?*"

Yasmine decided to ignore the other stuff and answered her question. "I'm staying at Michlifen Resort and Spa."

"Oooh, fancy."

They weren't going to be here up to a full day, so she had no idea why Kojo booked this place. They'd checked in an hour earlier and she'd taken a mini tour and saw the beautiful grounds. There was a fire pit beside the lounge chairs at the back. There was also a great size swimming pool, two restaurants and a gift shop, boutique and tea salon/coffee house. The rooms were simply amazing. Being that she hadn't planned on staying anywhere overnight, she had to make do with what was available in the boutique.

"You see, it's not that bad. Pull out your Kindle and enjoy the evening or better yet, enjoy Kojo. I know he's there with you." Salma giggled.

"Please don't talk him up. He's been surprisingly quiet, and I want it to stay that way."

"Wow, I never thought I'd see the day that first, you and Kojo wouldn't be all over each other, or second, the day you'd be running scared."

"The former is water under the bridge. The other thing you said, I'm not even going to deal with."

"What's the story with his son? The internet just says he's divorced. I wonder if the boy's mom is still in the picture."

Yasmine had wondered herself, but refused to ask Kojo about it. That summer in London, she knew for a fact that he wasn't married. Neither was she, although Pierre had been getting impatient with her hesitation to commit. When she got back to Tweede Kans Cove that summer, she was hurt, disappointed and angry. She decided to stop living in the clouds and seriously give Pierre a chance.

She wasn't in love with him, but cared about him deeply. He offered her emotional stability and security, and could provide the one thing she craved – a family. Something she had dreamed about since she was sixteen, but the man in her sights was Kojo. After all, he made her a promise. Because of her childhood, she rebuffed attachments to anyone other than her family. But Kojo broke through her hard exterior, only to also let her down.

"Yas?"

"Yeah, I'm sorry. What's up?"

"You zoned out for a pretty minute."

"Yea, sorry. *madha qult*?"

"I was saying, this season's also one of joy and love. I believe that all of this is in God's grand design for you."

Yasmine shook her head. She believed in Jesus and had faith just like the next person, but she also believed she had a bigger say in how her life went. She'd since let go of the notion of providence. She made things happen through calculated strategies and plans.

"No, it's not. He's here to do a job. After that, he'll go on with his life and I with mine."

"*ymkn 'an tajealak tasheur bitahasun?*"

"Does what make me feel better?"

"Holding on to the hurt and pain? To keep up this closed off façade so nothing will be able to hurt you. Sis, hurting is a part of life. Pain and pleasure – you have to give a little room to enjoy the abundance of the life we've been promised in Christ. This season should be a reminder of that. I know bad things happened, but get over it," Salma fussed.

"I'm here, aren't I?" Yasmine yelled back.

"You're here in body, but not in spirit. Anisa notices, you know? My niece is as smart as a whip. She sees how grudgingly uptight you are. You're spending the Christmas with us, but not really. To you, it's about that stupid benefit and accomplishing another goal. It's supposed to be about friends, family, fellowship and all-around love, peace, joy and hope. Loosen up sis. Only then will the fine things of life come to you."

"You know I'm the big sister here?" Yasmine asked with a smile. Her baby sister had just read her the riot act. Although it pained her to admit, there wasn't a false statement in what she'd said.

Salma laughed. "And I love you, but you're not acting like it. It hurts all of us to see you like this. We've been quiet for years, but enough is enough. We're all we have. You generally don't like Christmas because of the memories, but you're are stuck up all year round."

"Okay, I get it. I'll be more present. But that has nothing to do with Kojo. That man hurt me, and I have no intention of dealing with him again."

"And you don't have to. Just forgive him and move on."

"Gotcha." Yasmine let out a deep breath. She needed to process everything her baby sister had said, but for now, was ready to move the conversation on to lighter things. "So, I'm never home during Christmas. What happens?"

For the next couple of minutes, Salma told her sister of all the things her family did for Tweede Kans Cove during the Christmas season, reminding Yasmine of traditions she'd subconsciously placed at the back of her mind. Minutes later, the sisters said their goodbyes.

Just when Yasmine picked up the remote to find something on TV, there was a knock at her door. She hadn't ordered anything and Kojo had retired so at eight pm, she had no idea who it could be. She walked to the door and looked through the peephole but saw nothing. As she turned, the knock came again. She opened the door. Smiling down at her was Kojo. In his hand was a basket.

"You promised me food and a talk. Let's go."

She frowned and looked down at her attire. She had on grey leggings and a burgundy caftan with a grey cashmere cover up. Her face was bare, and her hair was in a bun. Compared to his matching, multi-print, Ziedu original lounge wear, she looked terrible.

Kojo must have read her thoughts because when her eyes met his again, he shrugged. "What? You're beautiful and you're the one that said you're not dressing up. So, let's go."

Salma's words popped into her head and she sized him up. "No need to be bossy. Let me put on some shoes."

As she turned away, he laughed. "Being anything less will have me reading Christmas stories to old people next, so there's a need. Now, come on."

Yasmine couldn't help the smile that spread across her face. She picked up her keycard and phone and walked out of the room.

# CHAPTER 11

"I thought I was okay, but I wasn't," Kojo explained.

Kojo had spent the last few hours setting this up. While Yasmine waited for Mr. Buttatu, the flurries intensified. From what he remembered of Ifrane; the weather was nice, but seriously unpredictable. And even at that, the town was rarely prepared for snow on the roads. He had called the hotel he knew about, and after a few promises and money exchanging hands, he had the chef prepare them a four-course meal which he asked them to pack up. He'd had the lounge closed so it would just be the two of them. Currently, they were on the two-seater sofa, in front of the burning fire pit. Their dinner was spread out before them. Since the area wasn't covered, he also had two blankets, one which was now draped across Yasmine's shoulders and the other over their legs.

The feeling Kojo got sitting this close to her was indescribable. He had taken off the tie she used to hold up her hair and let the wavy mass fall on her shoulders. She was so beautiful. He picked up the bottle of wine he had chilled, twisted off the cap and poured it into plastic flutes. He handed her one, trying to figure out how to explain things to her. He didn't want to scare her, knowing how she had the tendency to over analyze. He decided on simplicity.

"When my uncle came to get me, he took me to Ghana. That's how I got to know my mother's people. I still have no idea who my dad is and at this point, I'm okay not knowing. Where I come from in Ghana, Fante, we're matrilinear, so it's all good."

"What does that mean?" she asked.

"It means unlike typical Africans that claim where their dad is from, I claim where my mom is from."

She nodded but didn't respond.

"The more I got to know about my mother and her life – which was very comfortable might I add – the more enraged I became. How could she just throw me away in Tweedes and continue with her life? It wasn't until she was about to die that she confessed to my uncle. That was the only way he found me. Incidentally, I was looking for them too."

Kojo took a sip of his drink and set the flute down. The only other person he told his true feelings to was his therapist. "Yas, if the person that gave me life could abandon me and go about her life so effortlessly without a care in the world, what does that say about me?"

He really wasn't expecting her to answer and was kinda glad she didn't. She did reach out to squeeze his hand. The contact sent shock waves through his body and he was sure hers as well because she abruptly removed her hand. He stared at her and their eyes locked. He so badly wanted to kiss her, but there was still a lot to be said.

"It took a while with immigration and stuff, and then my uncle took me to the U.S where he was based. It's there I went to college. I wanted to keep in contact – I promise I did. But my life with him in the U.S. was so new to me and the only thing I knew to do with all I was feeling was shut down. I ended up getting into a lot of trouble."

Kojo narrated his college years and run ins with the law. Nothing major and thankfully, his uncle was patient with him.

Yasmine asked how he came into music. He told her the story of how he accompanied his uncle, who was an accountant, to the office of one of his clients who happened to be a big-time music producer. Kojo had always played the guitar and had a natural knack for music. So the guy took him under his wings for about two years. That experience gave him the leverage he needed. Kojo started touring and growing in the industry. It was right after the incident in London that he met the guys of the 891 crew.

"So, you've been doing this for about twelve years now?" she asked.

"Yes. Yas, I'm so sorry about shutting you out. I deeply regret London and I'm sorry. The more I thought about my mother's abandonment, the easier it was to distrust the love any woman had for me. How could they love me when the one who birthed me didn't? I'm not making excuses, but this is my truth."

"But you got married? Had a son? Weren't you in love?" Her voice was soft. The last thing he wanted was her pity. However, the hint of challenge in her tone had him inwardly jumping for joy. It meant that underneath this façade, she cared. Kojo stifled his smile.

"The thing with Lydia and I was superficial. I respect her as the mother of my son, but it wasn't supposed to end in marriage. We dated off and on for years. To quench my pain, I dabbled in drugs, alcohol and meaningless sex. The fame didn't help either, although I was never too far gone for my coping mechanism to be noticed. I functioned very well. It wasn't until I had a fatal accident that killed one of my acquaintances and had me in the hospital for a month that I decided, something had to give."

"Oh my God." Yasmine scooted closer to him and gave him an unexpected hug.

Kojo savored the comfort of being in her arms. Her perfume sent him on a euphoric high. He didn't know how much he needed her touch until this moment. Earlier he had convinced himself that if she wanted nothing to do with him after this, he would just leave. Now, that was no longer an option. He needed

Yasmine in his life. He might have done without her physically over the years, but not once did his heart leave hers.

Moments later she pulled back and Kojo mourned the loss of her warmth. But she didn't move back to her former sitting position. She stayed close to him.

"When I recovered, I first gave my life to Christ. Although the 891 Crew is a gospel band and I'm their keyboard player and producer, I didn't live for Christ. I started going to therapy and decided to take my Ghanaian surname. Before all this, Lydia became pregnant. Out of obligation and me thinking as a renewed Christian I had to do right by her, I married her. She had my son. We tried to make it work but it just didn't. My heart was somewhere else, and she had her own agendas. For some reason she thought vows would keep me from music." He sighed. He thought of the numerous fights they had any time he announced he had to leave on tour or took on a new client in another country.

Yasmine sipped her wine and lifted a forkful of the mini *m'banncha* Kojo had ordered for dessert. When he placed the order, he prayed the flaky, sweet, filo pastry was still her favorite. It was stuffed with almond frangipane with a subtle hint of rose water. Judging from her moan, his prayer was answered.

They'd had lamb tagine, couscous, and kesra. During dinner, he kept the conversation light. They discussed, politics, the benefit and Grand Amour. She asked him questions about the band, all general topics. He didn't expect her to chat so openly with him. This Yasmine was different from the person who stomped into the hotel elevator when it became evident they wouldn't be returning to Tweede Kans Cove.

"So how long have you been divorced?"

"Four years."

"That's how long Pierre has been gone."

As selfish and stupid as it had been, he remembered calling all those years ago and Mustafa telling him she went out with the Pierre dude. Mustafa, not knowing the depth of his feelings for

Yasmine, was very free with the amount and depth of the information he offered. Even their probable wedding. It was sometime after Yasmine left London that summer. Kojo remembered being so angry although he had no right to be. How could his life be falling apart, and she was thinking of getting married?

"Tell me about him. Did you love him?"

Her eyes connected with his briefly then she broke contact. Staring into the burning fire, she shrugged. "Honestly, I don't know. He was a gentleman, kind, compassionate. The only thing I couldn't stand was his heavy reliance on his family's name. It's as though he expected people to clear the way when he told them his name." She chuckled.

Kojo knew that she and her siblings, on the other hand, hesitated to tell people who they were. Their formative years were spent borderline poor. The twins were already eight when they moved to Tweedes. They weren't born with a silver spoon. But the one they were handed, they had a hard time accepting.

"I cared for Pierre a lot. I don't think he was in love with me either. At least he couldn't have been."

Kojo frowned. "Why would you think that?"

"We were in our third year of marriage and Anisa was almost two when he died in a crash. Kicker was, he was found with a female companion." Yasmine let out a bitter chuckle. "I never knew about her. But you know small towns; your business is everyone's business. So, I got to learn that they were childhood sweethearts. The extent of their relationship, I refused to find out. The mere fact that where his car was found wasn't where he told me he was going before he left, spoke volumes."

"I'm sorry, Yas." That was the only thing he thought to say.

She chuckled again. The sound lacked humor but was laced with cynicism and regret. "For a long time, I blamed you..."

He wanted to ask why, but decided against interrupting.

"I longed for you for years. Every time I reached out, you pushed me away. It was like all the things we said and shared as teenagers didn't even happen. The last time in London was the last straw. I came home and got married as expected. Pierre provided what I'd come to terms that I really needed."

"What's that?"

"Stability and security. Love has nothing to do with that. It's a fleeting emotion that has the potential to destroy. It destroyed my mom, almost destroyed my grandparents because their only child chased after it, and then it caused me years of anguish because I thought I felt it for you. In the end, although Pierre's betrayal hurt, my heart was somehow spared because I went into the union with clearer eyes."

Kojo's heart constricted hearing those words pour from her lips. Not just because of him, but to hear her view on love and the effort she put into ensuring she never felt it. Not knowing what to say, he pulled her to him. Her head rested on his chest. They remained silent. The only sound you could hear was the crackling of the fire before them.

"I'm so, so sorry, Yas," he whispered.

She grunted.

He pulled away from her, cupping her face in his hands. Her eyes remained closed. "Look at me Yasmine." A beat later, her eyes met his.

"Baby, again, I'm sorry but I couldn't love you the way you deserved or trusted you loved me. I never stopped loving you, but I wouldn't have done right by you. Think we're damaged now? We would've been destroyed if we had entered any form of a relationship before we were healed. Love isn't at all how you describe it and I know I contributed to your outlook."

He paused when she looked away from him. "Yas baby, I need you to look at me when I say this." He waited while she continued to look downwards. Seconds passed, then he lifted her face with his index finger.

"I never stopped loving you. Our experiences and stuff we went through brought us back to this moment. Give me a chance to take your hurt away. To show you that you have love pegged all wrong. Just like I've had to find out."

Yasmine removed his hand from her face and began to shake her head.

"Come on Yas, don't make me beg. I will though."

"Kojo, love and I don't agree. I'm fine with that now." She looked around. She gestured to the Christmas decorations. The hotel had gone all out Morocco style; with festive hanging floor lanterns, crystal and pearl beaded gold garlands, and rose gold ball string lights. "It's this season; it gives the false illusion of things unattainable."

He was irritated. How could the girl he knew turn out to be such a cynic? Was this her defense or coping mechanism?

"What's your problem with Christmas?" he asked. He knew her mom had passed some days before Christmas, but she had gotten over that, or so he thought.

Yasmine rubbed the back of her neck, then shrugged.

"Stop all that shrugging. Talk to me," he snapped.

Her eyes widened and she moved away from him. He saw her get ready to speak, but he raised his brow to her, daring her to say anything smart. She knew what was up and kept mute. Instead she sighed and returned her gaze to the burning fire.

Kojo pulled on his beard. "Come here."

She ignored him.

"Come here, Yas. Don't make me get up from here," he warned.

"You left Kwame back in Tweedes. You have no child here."

"I can't tell. I thought we were talking. After all we've shared you decide to clam up?"

She rolled her eyes and that did it. He stood and walked over to her. Kojo picked her up, dragging her blanket along and went back to his seat.

"Put me down, Kojo," she tried to wiggle away from him, but his hold was tight.

"Talk to me." He held her tightly in his lap.

"Will you let me go?"

"You have no bargaining power. I gave you a chance to come to me willingly. Why do you keep forgetting who I am?"

She rolled her eyes again.

He chuckled. "Keep rolling, they'll soon get stuck. Now talk to me."

She let out a deep breath. "The season just holds bad memories. Memories I hate being reminded of."

"I know about your mom. What else has you so mad at Christmas?"

"When did you leave?"

Kojo thought about it. It was about two weeks before Christmas. He bowed his head, placing it on her shoulder. He was so excited about his uncle coming back then, that he completely forgot that around that time, she became sad. He'd always been with her.

"My mom died around Christmas, and you left during the same time of the year." She sneered. "Pierre even died some days after Christmas. The season doesn't come with good memories, so I don't deal with it."

"So, you leave every Christmas?"

"Yes."

He held her tighter. Her shoulders began to shake a little and he could hear light sobs. He rubbed her back as she cried. From his own experience with grief and pain, he knew to let her get it all out. Knowing her, she probably hadn't let herself cry in years. Moments later, she lifted her head.

"You okay?"

Yasmine sniffled and gave a weary smile. "Yes KJ, I'm fine."

"Yes, there is a God." Kojo looked upward. "Thank you, Big Guy."

"What's wrong with you?" She looked puzzled.

He kissed her cheek. "You called me KJ."

Yasmine's cheeks turned red with a deep blush. She turned away from him.

"No, don't be shy now. I love it! So, you gonna give me a

chance to make it up to you? All my wrongs. They can't be wiped clean, but I'll make up for them."

"Kojo, we—"

He wasn't going to give her the chance to overthink. "No, just listen to me. We have ten days until Christmas Day. Be open. Give me a chance to show you the true meaning of this season."

She studied him. "I don't know..."

"You have nothing to lose. Do you? I mean it's not like you love me or anything. So, let me be your friend again."

Kojo knew what he had just told her was nothing but lies. He was aiming for her heart before he left Tweede Kans Cove. But he was going to let Yasmine think she was in control. That would be the only way to get her to loosen up and he, with the help of God, would work his magic.

"Or are you scared to be my friend because you have feelings for me?" he taunted.

"No, I don't have feelings for you. That ship has long sailed," she said in defiance, her tone an octave higher.

"Okay then, what do you say?"

"Okay, friends, starting now."

He shook his head. "One minute. We'll start after this."

"After wh—"

His lips captured hers. Kojo heard her gasp at the contact, but he didn't move away. Instead he deepened the kiss, allowing him to taste the red wine still on her lips. Her hands went to the nape of his neck and a prickly sensation travelled up his spine. He felt at home, a feeling he didn't want to end.

He had ten days to change her perception about Christmas and hopefully reawaken the love he knew she kept hidden within. Failure wasn't an option. No longer was reminiscing over the moments of what could've been all those years ago acceptable. Kojo was committed to making new memories and basking in now and hope of the future.

# CHAPTER 12

*K*ojo: *Hey! We still on for 2day?*
Yasmine: *Hey you! Yes.*
Kojo: *Great. We'll see you later.*

Yasmine reread the exchange she and Kojo had earlier. She absently caressed her bottom lip with the pad of her thumb. It'd been two days since Kojo placed his lips on hers and the feeling still lingered. When they got back from Ifrane, he made her promise to remain open. She did, but also knew she had to stay guarded. After Christmas was over then what?

Kojo had the potential to wrap her in euphoric heaven and then drop her without notice. She was no longer the sixteen-year-old or the college freshman or the master graduate who somehow couldn't let go of her first love. She was a thirty-four-year-old, single mother with a career she loved very much. She would be more open, not just as a promise to him, but for her daughter who seemed so happy with all the Christmas festivities.

She hadn't seen Kojo or Kwame since they'd gotten back from Ifrane. She'd been tied up at Grand Amour, attending to matters of the resort and wrapping up loose ends for the benefit. He had spent most of the time with Ms. Bernadette and her brothers.

Thinking of her brothers, Yasmine shook her head. She had

gone over to Omar's cottage to let him have it about cancelling on her at the last minute. He had the nerve to tell her he did her a favor, then proceeded to assuage her anger with a promise of a catered meal. She was going to make sure she collected on that promise.

"Mummy, are you listening?"

Anisa's voice interrupted her reverie. Yasmine looked down at the batter she was absently mixing and frowned. It was ready and she was about to whip it to death. She looked back up at her daughter.

"I'm sorry, angel, what did you say?" Yasmine walked over to the fridge and took out the eggs, sausages and butter.

"I was telling you that me and Kwame had a lot of fun with Aunty Salma yesterday."

"Really? Remind me again what you did." Yasmine placed the items on the island and unhooked the skillet from the overhead pot rack. She stopped moving and faced Anisa.

"We sang Christmas carols and made cards that we're going to send to those in jail. We also decorated our own small Christmas trees." Her daughter counted the activities off on her fingers in a sing song manner. Then she took a breath.

"That's great. So, are you excited to be spending Christmas at home?"

"Yes, Mummy, so much. But I'm a little sad though."

Yasmine frowned and turned on the water to rinse the skillet before placing it on the stove. "Why?"

"Because, Nana's house looks like Christmas, outside looks like Christmas, the resort looks like Christmas, but our house just looks the same." The little girl pouted her lips, twirling her ponytail.

Yasmine looked around the open layout of the cottage. No one would know that Christmas was eight days away. She never decorated because they were never here. After she realized they would be spending Christmas in Tweedes this year, she had been too busy with the benefit and the resort to even think about it.

"Well, guess what?"

"What?"

Yasmine giggled at the anticipation in her daughter's eyes.

"What Mummy? What?" Anisa pushed the iPad away from her and gave Yasmine her full attention.

"Uncle Kojo and Kwame are coming over and we're going to go shopping for a tree and decorations."

"Yaaay!" Anisa jumped down from the stool she was sitting on by the island and ran to her. "You're the best mummy ever."

Yasmine's throat clogged with emotion as she picked her daughter up. Was this what she had been depriving her daughter of by running away? "And you are the best daughter a mother could ever have." She kissed her forehead and put her down.

Yasmine glanced over at the rose and lily bouquet sitting in a vase she had brought home from work the day before. Kojo had sent them over. When she got the floral arrangement, her heart pounded to an erratic rhythm – a reaction she'd trained her heart to forget. She sighed and smiled moving her body to the melody of John Legend's rendition of "Silver Bells" as she continued to prepare breakfast. The doorbell rang some minutes later.

"Is that them?" Anisa asked, looking up from her device.

Yasmine wiped her hands with a paper towel. "I think so. Stay here and don't touch anything." She walked to the door, checked the peep hole. Beaming, she opened the door. The father and son pair wore matching outfits – blue jeans, light brown sweaters and peanut butter colored Timberlands on their feet.

"Hey, don't you look handsome," Yasmine said, stepping aside to allow them to enter.

"Thank you, you look lovely as always," Kojo replied, setting her body on fire with his gaze.

"Thanks, Kojo, but I was talking to Kwame." Yasmine smiled down at the little boy who had his father's good looks.

"Good morning, Ms. Yasmine," Kwame greeted.

"Good morning, baby. Are you ready to eat?"

Kwame nodded as Anisa came running down the foyer.

"Good morning, Uncle Kojo," Anisa greeted.

"Good morning, beautiful."

"Okay, Anisa take Kwame and turn on cartoons. Breakfast will be served soon."

As the kids ran away, Kojo's arm snaked around her waist, pulling her to him. "You got jokes huh?" He kissed her forehead.

"Whatever do you mean, Mr. Sarbah?" Yasmine removed herself from his hold. "Are these for me?" She motioned toward the bouquet in his hand.

"Nope. I brought them here because I felt like carrying something."

She gave him a sideways glance. "Ugh...you get on my nerves."

"Yeah that's what your mouth says." He grabbed her hand. "Come feed me, woman. I need all my energy to deal with you all day."

"Are you complaining?" she teased.

"Nope. Not at all."

An hour later, the four of them were fed and Yasmine was in her room changing her clothes. She smiled at the chatter coming from the kitchen as Kojo and the kids cleaned up. Glancing at herself again in the mirror, Yasmine nodded in satisfaction at her simple denim ensemble. She picked up her keys, fanny pack and left the room.

*Y*asmine watched Kojo as he surveyed a six-foot tree. It was the sixth tree they had looked at and she was ready to go. Glancing over and seeing the kids having fun running around the Tweedes Tree Farm was the only thing keeping her in place.

"KJ, if you bypass this tree for another one, I'm leaving you right here. I promise," she warned.

"I was wondering when you would show." He laughed. "I found our tree three trees ago."

She gave him a light punch on his shoulder. "Are you serious? And you kept me walking around this place."

"Loosen up. Go with the flow, baby. I got this." He looked around and quickly pecked her lips. Then took her hand and walked toward the front of the tree farm.

She smiled. "Erm, I think you have the concept of friendship mixed up. You haven't stopped kissing me since we left the house."

"I don't see you pushing me back." He winked at her as he gave the attendant instructions on the tree they had picked out. "Besides I read somewhere that kissing friends were the best kind of friends."

Yasmine laughed. "And where did you read that?"

Kojo placed his index finger on his lips and looked upward in contemplation.

She bumped him with her shoulder. "You're so silly."

"I'm telling you I read it. I just can't remember where, but if you give me a kiss, I'm sure I'll remember." He placed both hands on her waist.

Yasmine swatted his hands away. "Stop that. Everyone can see you."

Kojo shrugged. "I'm not worried."

"Well, you should be. We aren't kids anymore. One picture of you in the wrong hands and we'll be all over the entertainment news."

"As long as I'm pictured with you," he teased.

Yasmine shook her head and turned. "Be serious KJ." She walked toward the kid friendly patch to get the kids.

"Hey, wait up, Yas. I know you're not mad," he questioned.

"No, I'm not. But at the same time, I don't want to give people the wrong idea."

She smiled at the attendant who'd finished tying the tree to the roof of the truck. "Anisa, Kwame, let's go." The kids came running while Kojo leaned toward her ear. His breath sent shivers down her spine and goosebumps up her arms.

"Okay, I'll behave outside. Once we're indoors, it's fair game." He opened the door for her, then buckled the kids in and went around to get into the driver's seat. "So where to next, guys?"

"To buy the decorations!" both kids yelled.

Yasmine looked back at them and chuckled. They'd quickly taken a liking to each other. Yasmine had watched them off and on all day. Anisa wasted no time telling Kwame what to do and in turn Kwame showed how protective he was of her by not allowing any other boys to play with her. Anyone who didn't know them would think they were siblings.

*Siblings.* For a quick second Yasmine got lost in the thought. Then she shook her head and turned back around in her seat. Her eyes locked with Kojo's and he winked at her. He started the car, turned on the radio and the kids started singing along to, "Jingle Bells."

"Go with the flow, baby. Go with the flow."

Yasmine didn't respond because there wasn't an intelligible response she could give. There was no way he could've known what she was thinking. She inwardly chided herself. Kojo would be leaving the day after Christmas. She had to keep reminding herself of that. The flowers, kisses, sporadic sweet texts would all come to an end soon. They lived in completely different worlds.

# CHAPTER 13

"*A*nd we are done!" Kojo announced as he placed the angel on top of the tree.

"Do you guys want to turn on the lights?" Yasmine asked, steadying the ladder for him to climb down.

The kids shouted their yes.

"Okay, pack up these remaining decorations, then we'll turn on the lights at the count of three," she instructed.

As the kids were packing up, Kojo lifted Yasmine's face and quickly brushed his lips against hers. She frowned up at him and he chuckled. He loved kissing her, plain and simple. He knew she enjoyed it too, but the control freak in her wouldn't allow her to relax.

"What? It's been four hours since my last fix. I'm trying," he whispered. At least he thought he whispered.

"Your last fix of what, daddy?" Kwame asked.

"Yea, your last fix of what Kojo?" Yasmine stuck her tongue out at him and joined Anisa, who was still picking up the leftover decorations.

"Erm, my last fix of something sweet," Kojo responded.

Kwame frowned. "Did you eat our sugar cookies? I thought we were going to eat them after this?"

*No, I'm trying to bag my lifetime sugar supply.*

"I didn't eat your cookies, buddy," Kojo answered. "Is this ready?" He pointed to the box that had all the spare decorations. Yasmine nodded. He saw her struggling to stifle her laughter at the awkward moment he'd just had with Kwame. He picked up the box and took it to the storage room she pointed him to.

As he walked away from them, he heard them chattering about their day. After leaving the tree farm, they made their way to the store. They got decorations and baking ingredients because the kids begged to make cookies. After that, they had gone out to eat and came back to Yasmine's cottage. They baked a batch of cookies together and the kids took a nap. Once they woke up, they started to decorate the tree.

Kojo leaned on the door frame of the kitchen and observed the three people he loved dearly interact. Anisa was putting the cookies on a plate, while Kwame held the napkins and Yasmine balanced the cups of mint tea, cocoa and milk on a tray.

After the first day of observation, Kwame had opened up to the DuBois-Arazis. Grandma Olly made sure he called her Nana and Yasmine's siblings spoiled him as well. The day he and Yasmine got stuck in Ifrane, Kwame and Anisa had both slept at Salma's house. His son couldn't stop talking about all the fun things he and Nisa, as he called Anisa, had done.

*Jesus, this is what I long for. I know with Yasmine, I have my work cut out for me. But this Christmas season, do me a solid and soften that woman's heart.*

"If you're done daydreaming, we could use your presence," Yasmine said.

Kojo walked to her and took the tray from her. "Don't you want to know what I was daydreaming about?"

She studied him for a moment, and glanced back at the kids who were setting up around the tree. She turned back to him and shook her head. "With that look on your face, nope."

"Your loss, baby."

"Somehow I doubt that."

"Come on, Mummy, we're ready," Anisa yelled.

"Yes, Mummy, come on," Kojo mimicked.

Yasmine rolled her eyes at him. "So childish."

He laughed at her. He was going to loosen her up and win her over if it was the last thing he did.

"When God sent the angel to tell Mary that she'd give birth to Jesus, God already knew, and Jesus too, what His mission would be on earth," Kojo explained.

"He knew He would die and still He was doing good for other people?" Kwame asked.

"Yes, Kwame. Right, Uncle Kojo?" Anisa responded.

"Right Baby Girl."

"Noel" played softly from the Pandora streaming service as the four of them gathered around the lit Christmas tree. The cookies and beverages were long gone and Kojo had just finished reading and explaining Luke 18. It was something he'd been doing with Kwame since he talked to Ms. Bernadette.

On the way back from Ifrane two days ago, he asked Yasmine if she and Anisa would join them. It was his desire that the four of them would come together every day and read the Book of Luke. Explaining to the kids the life and deeds of Jesus would bring new, appreciated meaning to Christmas. He loved the idea when Ms. Bernadette shared it with him.

Kojo looked over at Yasmine. Her mood was pensive. She stared absently at the flames in the fireplace, deep in thought.

He gathered from the way she talked while they were in Ifrane that her relationship with Jesus needed repair. Kojo knew she still agreed with the moral guidelines of Christianity, as she strived to be a good person. But good people don't get into heaven; saved people do.

"Yas, you okay?"

She looked at the kids and he saw the exact moment her façade when back up. "Yes, I'm good."

There were so many things he wanted to say to her, but the audience they had told him it wasn't the right time. He had to find a way to get her alone. He wasn't going to allow her to reconstruct the wall she had gradually let down the past couple of days.

"Okay let's pray. Hold each other's hand," Kojo instructed.

Yasmine placed hers in his and he squeezed, forcing her to look at him. Their gazes locked and he searched them for some inkling of what she was thinking. When he got nothing, he redirected his attention to the task at hand.

"Eyes closed, head bowed. Dear Father, as Your children, we cry out for a fresh filling, and a new awareness of Who You are. We choose by faith to be examples, so others can see us as lighted trees of life, pointing to You this Christmas. You're our joy and peace. You are Lord of lords and King of kings. And we celebrate You as Lord—this Christmas and always. In Jesus' name," Kojo concluded.

"Amen!" Anisa and Kwame yelled in unison while Yasmine whispered it.

"All right guys, I'm going to help Yas clean up the kitchen and wash up. Straighten up here. Buddy, when I'm done, we'll leave. It's been a long day."

After moments of moving in silence in the kitchen, Kojo trapped Yasmine between the island and his body. She refused to meet his eyes.

"Look at me, Yas."

She didn't acknowledge his command.

"Yas, look at me." Her eyes found his. He lifted his hand to tuck a lose tress behind her ear. "You shut down in there. Talk to me."

Yasmine hesitated.

"We're friends, right?"

She nodded.

"So, tell me what's up?"

"Nothing really. I was just reflecting on the teaching from Luke. Especially the part about persistent prayer. I've been hurting and angry for so long that I don't even know what true prayer feels like anymore. I mean I say the words but…"

"Baby, I know exactly what you mean. And me too. When God saved me in that accident, I came to the realization that for so long, my claim to Christianity was superficial. Even as a producer of Christian music. Hurt, pain and anger I refused to address were roadblocks to any relationship I desired to have with the Lord," Kojo said.

A lone tear rolled down her cheek. "I've somehow traded my spiritual beliefs for truth grounded in anything other than faith."

"There's hope. That is, after all, the reason for the season, right? And I'm here to guide you along the way. We'll figure this thing out together."

"For how long though? KJ, I have—"

Kojo lifted his index finger to her lips to silence her. "Come on, Yas. Let's just go with the flow. One thing I do promise you is I'm never letting you go again." He made sure he kept eye contact with her so she could see how serious he was.

There were a lot of obstacles in their path. Their jobs, the kids, distance. But one thing he knew for sure. Yasmine DuBois-Arazi was never getting away from him. The thought was like a vice around his heart. He wouldn't survive. He knew that. Now all he had to do was make sure she knew it, too.

# CHAPTER 14

"*H*ow didn't I know you guys did this every year?" Yasmine whispered to her sister. "You left this out."

Salma glanced at her. "My bad. We started a couple of years ago—"

"Yep, I think it was the first year you developed your wings." Omar wiggled his brow.

"*la tabda maei*," Yasmine warned. "Don't start."

Mustafa turned around. "Shhhh."

Yasmine cocked her head to the side.

"Yeah, you. I'm shushing you," he answered her unspoken challenge.

Salma and Omar snickered. Their theatrics were cut short when Grandma Olly cut her eyes at them.

The four siblings stood behind their grandmother as she gave a speech to the servicemen and women of Tweede Kans Cove. Yasmine knew her grandparents had a soft spot for policemen and firefighters, considering their grandfather's brother was a firefighter. She also knew that every year, her grandparents contributed to the one and only fire house and police department in Tweede Kans Cove.

What she didn't know was when they started giving away Christmas baskets. When her siblings barged into her office earlier, pulling her along, she was excited, but now she was kind of sad. She felt like an outsider. Had she been so stuck in her victimhood that she totally blocked out her family at this time of the year? It was as though she had no idea what they did. In years past, when she returned, she begged them to spare her the details.

"It's time, Yas, come on," Mustafa told her, jerking her out of her thoughts.

"What are we doing now?" she asked, but didn't get a response since her brother had walked ahead of her to the back table. Salma and Omar were on the opposite side of the room while their grandmother socialized.

For the next hour, they handed out Christmas baskets and vouchers for the recipients' choice of goose or beef. She smiled, greeted and engaged in small talk as each person walked up to the table to accept the gifts on behalf of the DuBois family. Her phone chimed in her pocket and she retrieved it, already knowing who was on the other end. She smiled, looking into her phone, as her guess proved right.

Kojo: ***Hey Beautiful. How is it going? U done?***

***Just about. Are you guys having fun?*** She texted back.

Since the day of the tree lighting, she and Kojo had grown closer. Almost inseparable. In the last four days, they talked throughout the day. He had flowers delivered to her office every mid-morning. Then he'd stop by to take her to lunch or bring lunch to her.

For the first time in years, on his insistence, she took advantage of the ski area the town had. He made it his duty to see she didn't work past three p.m. every day. Holiday hours, he called it. They went to the movies, park, the book café and the Jazz club. He had everything meticulously planned out, alternating the day the two of them spent alone and the days they spent with the kids.

Each night, he'd Facetime her and Anisa and read another chapter in Luke, building on the day before. They were now in chapter twenty-two. She was on Cloud Nine. And although she tried to remind herself each day not to get caught up, she found herself falling deeper into the abyss of love.

Her phone chimed again, signifying she'd received a response. Kojo: ***Yes. See you soon. Love you.***

Her heart skipped a beat as she read that. He had started telling her he loved her since that night in her house. However, she wasn't brave enough to utter the words and Kojo hadn't pressured her about her feelings. For that she was glad.

"So, I guess O and I are no longer on your hit list?" Mustafa asked.

Yasmine didn't need to turn around to know that her brother was smiling, something he rarely did. Along with their mother, Mustafa got several beatings from their father. He learned to mask the pain and still did. Yasmine knew that underneath that hard core, her brother was a big ol' teddy bear, but it would take a special woman to dig through the layers.

"You're just so nosy. Mind your business."

"You are my business. Until you remarry. Even then, your husband just has to get used to the fact that my sister will always be my business." Mustafa put his arm around her neck and kissed her temple. They walked to the rest of the family.

"You do know your hand is heavy?" she teased.

"Stop complaining. Answer my question. Are we off your hit list?"

Yasmine shrugged. "What do you want me to say, Musa?"

Mustafa stopped walking and turned her to face him. "I want you to say that you'll consider being happy. That you'll free yourself from this prison you've kept yourself in. I want you to say that you will, most of all, be truthful with yourself." He paused, probably expecting an answer from her, but she had nothing to give him. Her eyes darted behind him to see Omar, Salma and their grandmother engaged in conversation with the police chief.

"Yas, are you listening to me?"

"I hear you, Musa. But Christmas will soon be over. Reality

kicks back in. I'm enjoying now, but I'm not reading too much into it."

"I watched you pine over that man for years. I wanted to break his neck for having such a hold on you. I also listened to him when he called me last month pleading with me to help him," Mustafa said.

Yasmine wasn't ready to deal with this now so decided to get him away from her. She had the perfect way to do it. "You're giving out all this advice. What about you? Do you think we don't wanna see you happy?"

As she knew he would, Mustafa turned around and began strolling over to the others. Yasmine laughed at her big brother. "Come on, we were peeling back our layers, and having deep revelations here," she teased.

"Ha, ha. Very funny. Think about what I said or come the new year, I'm shipping you to another location. I'm done seeing you brooding around this place."

Yasmine continued to laugh and clutched her imaginary pearls. "Are you threatening me? I thought you were supposed to protect me?"

Mustafa stopped and turned to her. "I am protecting you... from yourself. *'ana ahbik ya 'ukhti*. Let me know when the guys get here." He pulled out his phone, ending the conversation.

Kojo had stayed back at Mustafa's with the kids. He had some business to take care of and offered to babysit. The 891 Crew would be arriving later in the evening and he wanted to get some things for the upcoming tour wrapped up. She smiled when she remembered him saying he wanted to be free to help her host them.

"Okay, I love you family, but I have to run. The band's flight should be arriving in five hours and I need to make sure the driver gets going." Yasmine adjusted the strap of her bag on her shoulder.

"I'm proud of you, Yasmine. And I know your grandfather would've been too," her grandmother said.

Yasmine lowered her eyes briefly, blinking to hold back tears. She missed her grandfather deeply and often wondered how her grandmother coped. "Thank you, grandma."

Grandma Olly looked around, and shook her head. "Omar, come take me home." She hollered out and put on a fake smile for the young woman Omar was talking to. They watched as Omar whispered in the lady's ear and scurried over to them.

"Hey old lady, why are you trying to mess up my flow?" Omar said, kissing their grandmother on her cheek.

"How will any woman take you seriously when they are all games to you?" Grandma Olly asked.

Yasmine and her sister chuckled with their arms folded across their chests, waiting on his reply. Mustafa had walked out when a call came through.

"Grandma, don't underestimate my charm." Omar turned his attention to his sisters. "What are y'all laughing at? Yas, don't you have someone to nag or be mad at? And Sal, shouldn't you be somewhere getting on somebody's nerves?" Without waiting for their responses, he put his arm around their grandmother. "Come on, my favorite lady. Let's get you home."

Yasmine looked at her sister, who nodded in unspoken agreement and immediately, they both hit him with their purses.

"Ouch, stop man, okay my bad. Jeez. In fact, I'm not cooking for the next week. Y'all gotta figure out how you're going to do Christmas dinner." He started to limp as though he was really hurt.

Yasmine and Salma looked at each other and started apologizing, but were still unable to stifle their laughter.

"Get off me." He shrugged them off. "Come on, grandma. Now I gotta go lay down."

Omar continued to fuss while their grandmother shook her head. Once they were outside, Mustafa came over to the car and frowned. "What's wrong with you?"

"Your violent sisters, man," Omar said. He opened the door

for their grandmother to get in and walked to the driver's side. "Better get them to cook for Christmas. I don't feel good."

"Whatever O. Don't play with me. I'm looking forward to that roasted goose," Salma yelled out on her way to Mustafa's car.

"Then you better get to learning how to cook it," Omar shouted back.

Yasmine walked to her car laughing because she could still hear Salma grumbling about the roasted goose and how she would injure him if it wasn't ready Christmas Day. As she started the car, Yasmine giggled because the person her sister was fussing at was long gone. She brought out her phone and dialed.

"Wassup, Baby." Kojo's deep voice made her shiver when he answered.

"Hey KJ."

"I missed you today," he said.

"Today isn't over and I saw you this morning."

"You saw me for less than two minutes over Facetime. But you're right, today's not over. We're getting together later?"

She smiled as though he could see her. "Yes."

"I love it when you don't fight me so much."

"It's the season of giving. So, enjoy it while you can."

"Does that mean I can ask for something else?"

Yasmine rolled her eyes and let out a chuckle. "Go ahead."

Yasmine suddenly felt her throat getting dry at the words that Kojo spoke next. She opened her mouth to speak but words didn't come out. Instead she heard laughter from the other end of the line before he hung up.

"I like the guys."

Kojo glanced up at her, the fire he was making was temporarily forgotten as he tried to decide how much he should read into that declaration. He narrowed his eyes at her. "Don't get yourself into trouble, young lady."

Yasmine giggled. The sound stirred something deep within him. The more time they spent together, the more he realized that whatever he had with any other woman in the last eighteen years, paled in comparison to what he felt for Yasmine. His Yas. With each passing hour, each passing day, his heart strings pulled in a familiar direction. Could he take another rejection? He had it all figured out in his mind, but he knew with Yasmine, it might be a hard sale.

"What? I like them. Is that so bad. You seem closer to Adeniyi. How did you guys meet?" She asked, removing the items in the basket he had packed for them.

When he talked to her earlier, he asked her to come out to their cave with him. He was stunned when she said yes and quickly sprang into action. He adjusted the wood under the fire and rubbed his hands together, absorbing the heat.

He shrugged. "So, I told you about how my uncle introduced

me to some people in the industry. Well, one night hanging out, we went to this club where I met three Nigerian guys who blew me away with their sound. I went over to introduce myself to my fellow African brothers and the rest, you can say, is history."

Kojo moved closer to Yasmine and helped her unpack their dinner. The fire provided the ambiance he was going for. Comfortable and romantic. He stretched his legs out on the double blanket that was already laid out. They used to come to this cave as teenagers. Mostly to talk, but they did make out once or twice. Nothing too extreme as they were both deathly afraid of her grandmother and Ms. Bernadette. Kojo had always loved kissing Yasmine and that they did a lot. He turned around and grinned when he located their initials. The Y and the K they'd carved into the wall many years ago.

"So Adeniyi sings, then his brother raps and the other guy is on the drums. And you produce or is the correct term, lay beats?"

Kojo laughed. "You're so corny. But your run down is correct. I also write. Most of their award-winning songs, Niyi and I wrote. But we also have songwriters."

The next couple of minutes, he busied himself with setting up dinner and the game of mancala. He hoped they'd get to play later.

He'd accompanied the driver to get the guys. Once they returned, Yasmine and her siblings were on hand to welcome them. They were shown their accommodations and had decided to retire for the day. The following day, they'd be busy with preparing for the benefit and Kojo also wanted to take them on a tour of his town. So, he needed this uninterrupted time with Yasmine. He called in a favor with Salma for the kids to ensure they weren't disturbed.

The next several minutes over dinner, they continued to catch each other up on what had been happening in their lives since they'd been apart. Every day and time they talked revealed something new. Grand Amour and Anisa were Yasmine's favorite topics. The joy as she talked about her family's legacy was contagious. She tried to downplay her accomplishments, but he wouldn't let her.

He told her about his plans after active touring. He loved music and it would always be a part of him. But instead of traveling as much, he wanted to be more stable in Accra and produce more. He even planned on opening an academy to train upcoming artists. He asked God for a family and he was now more than ever, committed to doing whatever it took to make sure he had a stable, secure environment for them.

As it had always been, Yasmine expressed her unadulterated pride in him. Even all those years ago when subconsciously, he thought he didn't deserve to be loved, she always found a way to speak life into him.

"You've always gone after what you wanted and succeeded. I'm so happy for you, KJ, and proud," she gushed. Yasmine sat back and rubbed her stomach, full of their meal.

He watched and for a second, wondered what it would be like for her to carry a product of their love in there. He had Kwame and she had Anisa, but he wanted something they'd be able to share together.

"Thank you, Yas. I'm proud of you too. My little Yas."

"Boy, you wish. I haven't been your little anything since I was eleven and that's light years away."

"You can be my big Yas if that makes you feel better. As long as we're not messing with the '*my*' part." He winked.

Yasmine took a sip of her drink before responding. "And you call me corny. You're worse."

"Yeah, says the girl who can recite Meg Ryan's part in *When Harry Met Sally* almost verbatim," he said.

Her hand flew over her mouth. "Oh my God. You remember that? Well, I can't anymore."

"What do you mean? You don't watch those romantic chick flicks anymore?"

"Nope. Those movies are a set up. They make you believe that something like that really exists out there." She pulled out the mancala board. "You ready to lose?"

"You know you can't beat me. But hold on a second." Kojo frowned at her. "You don't believe love exists?"

"I just think too much is put into the jitters one feels in their stomach for the person they're attracted to," she said.

"But those jitters aren't love, Yas. You know that." Kojo drew her closer into his arms so her head rested on his chest while his back rested on a smooth boulder. He kissed her hair. "Love is commitment, love is sacrificial, love is forgiveness, and love is fighting and making up. God is love. Those jitters fade when the person does something you don't like because it quickly turns into anger or some other feeling. But love trumps all that."

"Love is also pain. It hurts." She sighed.

"But yeah, you're trusting another with the most fragile part of you. Your heart. It will hurt, but it's not supposed to hurt too much."

"Tell me about it," she murmured.

A part of him wanted to end this conversation here so they could go back to joking and jesting. However, he knew that now was as good a time as any to lay all his cards on the table. Christmas would soon be over, and he'd have to leave. He wanted no ambiguity between them. He wanted her to know exactly where he stood.

When Salma first called him weeks ago, all he did was regret the road he took that led him away from Yasmine. Now all he could do was thank God. Because that road led him back here. He had one goal in mind when he came to Tweede Kans Cove and that was to win back the love of his life.

"Sit up, Baby," he said.

Yasmine groaned, but then sat up and turned to him. Her eyes were hooded. He caressed her cheek with the back of his hand. The chemistry between them filled the atmosphere. Chemistry had never been their problem. It was the other facts of life that proved to be stumbling blocks.

He inhaled her scent. The words he intended to say were stuck in his throat. Her hazel eyes told him she felt the force between them too. He opened his mouth again to speak when her lips landed on his. She repositioned herself in his lap and snaked her arms around his neck. Kojo wrapped his arms around her waist. He held on for dear life as their lips tangoed.

All the memories of joy, misery, love and pain they had gone through together came flooding back. He was a boy dealing with the abandonment of the woman that was supposed to love him first. She was a girl who grew up in a volatile situation and blamed herself for her parents' demise. Even at that young age, they shared secrets, exposed their vulnerability and tried to help each other heal.

Yasmine moaned and he pulled back. She frowned and he pecked her lips once more. He had to break this up. They were getting carried away. He had been celibate since he became born again and he knew she hadn't had sex since her husband's death. In his own power, he wouldn't let them get that far. But dealing with Yasmine, nothing was in his power. She made him weak. He lost all sense, especially with her mouth on his.

*Father, help me. Where did she learn to kiss like that?* He tugged on his beard.

Yasmine wiped the corner of her lips and her brows furrowed. "What's wrong?"

"You've gotten really good. I don't know if I should be mad or thankful," he said, with a faint smile.

She lowered her eyes and her cheeks turned a mild shade of red. *Cute.*

"Baby, I love kissing you. But we need to talk."

"Whyyyyyyy? Why do you want to spoil this with words?"

Kojo laughed. "You know you look just like Anisa when you do that?"

"But I'm serious. Words complicate things."

"Then we're about to get super complicated because we need to talk."

"About what?"

Kojo frowned at her. "About us. What do you mean about what?"

"KJ, why can't we just enjoy now?"

Kojo cocked his head to the side and moved her off his lap. He didn't need any body contact with her now. *Was she serious?*

"Yasmine, I'm too old to just enjoy now. I've seen and gone through a lot in my thirty-six years. I know exactly what I want. I know you do too, behind this façade. Doesn't it get exhausting?"

"Kojo, I don't know what you want from me." She pulled the blanket up to her waist.

"Oh, I'm Kojo now?" He shook his head. "I want you to tell me what you feel, what you want. Since the first day I got here, I've gutted myself for you. I've exposed all my scars. I know I hurt you bad. I'm so sorry, babe. And I'll spend a lifetime making it up. But you gotta put down your walls and let me."

Kojo waited with bated breath for her to let him in. To show him an inkling of what she was feeling. If he didn't think she loved him, he wouldn't be trying to wear her down. The first day he laid eyes on her in Beautiful Eyes after eight years, he knew she did. He regretted rejecting her over and over all those years, but this was their future. He was counting on the miracle of the season.

Christ was born to give mankind a second chance. Kojo wanted a second chance with her. He was committed to fulfilling every promise he ever made to her, but in this moment, feared she wouldn't let him.

"I almost went crazy for you. My siblings teased me. My grandmother reprimanded me. How could I be sixteen and feel as deeply as I did? I don't know but I did. For two years you ignored me. You didn't even reach out. Then you did and it was to Mustafa. It was from him I got your number. You acted like you didn't promise to protect me, to always be there. You were so cold, like I was a stranger—"

"Ba—"

Yasmine held up her hand to him. "No, let me finish. Do you know what it felt like to be rejected by your best friend, your love, repeatedly? Then in London, you treated me like—"

"I know what I did Yas, please don't say it..." His heart ached.

She chuckled. "Why? I thought we are talking?" Sarcasm dripped from her tone.

"About the future—"

"That doesn't mean we forget the past," she challenged.

"But it also doesn't mean we become prisoners of it." Kojo let out a labored breath and took her hand in his. "Yasmine, I'll fulfill every promise I made to you...just let me."

Several beats passed between them, then she cupped his face with her soft palms. "I love you, Kojo..."

"I know that, Yas." He winked at her.

"Ugh, cocky much?"

"Not cocky, just stating the truth. But that's not in question, love. The question is will you let me love you?"

"We're not the same kids from back then. There are so many things to consider. You and I aren't in the same world. They call you Keyz, for goodness sake. You're an award-winning producer, a celebrity with women throwing themselves at you. Tweedes must have made you forget who you are. I'm just Yasmine."

"How many times do I have to tell you, not to shrink yourself...ever?"

She rolled her eyes. "I didn't mean it like that..."

"I don't care how you meant it. Don't do it." He paused. "I know who I am. The only woman I want throwing herself at me is you. Of course, we aren't those teenagers – thank God. I'm not asking you to be a part of my public world. I'm asking you to be a part of my life."

"Are they really any different?"

"Technically, no. But I do everything I can to keep them separate. I need you, Yas. Just give us a chance and we'll figure everything out as we go along."

"Promise?"

Kojo felt his heart bursting at the seams. "Cross my heart and hope to die..."

She hit him on his arm. "Don't say that."

"Ouch woman, I don't mean it literally. You're just about to give me a chance. I'm not trying to die."

"Hmmm. What are you trying to do then?"

"I plan on getting more sugar. Talk time is over." He signaled her over with his index finger. "Come here."

Yasmine scooted over to him and he tapped his lap for her to straddle. She did. He fastened his arms around her waist and looked into her eyes. "I love you, Yasmine Sarbah." He laughed at the shocked expression on her face.

"Calm down, scary. I'm just practicing. When I ask you to marry me, there'll be no doubt about my request. For now, you're giving me back your heart." He pecked her lips. "Get ready, I'm going to fulfill every promise I ever made to you."

Yasmine pressed her forehead against his. "You wanna know a secret?"

"Wassup?"

"I never took my heart back. It was broken, but you've always had possession."

The twinkle in her eye caused his heart to skip a beat. The words she'd just spoken punched him in the gut. "And I intend to heal and cherish it forever."

With that declaration, he captured her lips. She was eleven, he was thirteen. At that age, God gave him a gift he was too messed up to appreciate. He'd been given his second chance and he was never letting go.

"No, this can't be happening. How? There was no sign. None. But I should've known," Yasmine berated herself as she paced in her office.

"Sis, will you calm down? It's still noon. The benefit doesn't start until seven p.m. There's still time for it to clear up," Omar told her.

Yasmine shot her eyes toward him. She bit back what she really wanted to say. There was no reason for him to bear the brunt of her anger. All her rage belonged at Mother Nature's feet. Yes, her and Kojo.

*I can't even blame them. I allowed this to happen. I allowed myself to get caught up.*

"For the record, lil brother, never tell a woman to calm down. You'll get the exact opposite reaction," she said.

Omar grunted, but didn't look up from the laptop on his lap. He was trying to trace the food truck that was bringing items for the day's events. Even though he was a chef, he solely took care of the family and the resort. He wasn't in charge of catering the benefit, although he made recommendations for who they should go with.

"Now, this is unprecedented in the history of Ifrane and its neighboring town," the newscaster said.

"Yes, Imaan, I do agree. We have the occasional snowfall every holiday season. The last time we had people being shut in was almost ten years ago and that was with five inches of snow," the other anchor replied.

Yasmine gripped the remote and tapped her head gently with it.

"You're going to give yourself a headache with that thing," Mustafa said, coming through the door with Salma in tow.

Salma walked over to her and took the remote from her. "Give me that and stop panicking. The snow is in Ifrane now. There's a fifty percent chance it would get here."

"Stop telling her that. It will more than likely get here. What we need to do now, is figure out a contingency," Omar said.

"I should've been on it. I was on a call with Mr. Rafik about his hall in case the outside venue fell through..."

Yasmine allowed her words to trail off as she thought about her blunder. Tweede Kans Cove was cool, but not frigid, so she had championed the plan for the benefit to be outside. The band and other musical acts would be on stage, while food trucks and other activities would be on the side. Considering Tweede Kans Cove was a small town, her deputy and the committee wanted to give it a carnival feel, but at the same time, keep it classy and warm, with the spirit of Christmas running through. She'd agreed then.

What was she thinking? Once she took over, she should have gone with a more structured approach. The unpredictability of the weather had always been in the back of her mind. She even thought about the contingency plan in the event something did go wrong. However, for the past week and a half, she'd been so wrapped up in the euphoria of Kojo that she had dropped the ball. Some time last week, she got the initial sign that the weather might be a problem. She was on a phone call about an inside venue, but was placed on hold. A minute later, Kojo peeked his head through her doorway and practically forced her to go to lunch with him.

Yasmine placed her head in her hands. "Why didn't I remember?"

"Remember what?" Kojo walked into her office with his friend, Adeniyi.

Yasmine turned and her eyes did the exact opposite of what she wanted them to do. They took him in. As much as she tried, she couldn't snatch her eyes away from him. Heat prickled her skin, causing her to lick her lips. Warmth dripped over her as she admired his muscles that refused to remain hidden under the dark green hoodie he wore over black jeans. His nose ring and the diamond stud in his left ear sparkled like he'd just had them polished. Kojo winked at her and that snapped her back to reality. She rolled her eyes. If she hadn't been so caught up in that, she wouldn't be dealing with this.

Adeniyi had just finished greeting her siblings and walked over to her. "Hey Yas. Wassup?" he asked.

"The weather is threatening to turn the benefit into a disaster," she responded.

"Oh, he gets an answer and I get an eye roll?" Kojo asked.

She could hear the annoyance underneath his jest. He kissed her on her cheek and walked over to her brothers.

For the next couple of hours, Yasmine watched in horror as the meteorologist predicted dimmer weather. Her brothers, Kojo and Adeniyi talked about possible contingency plans as she was stuck in place. All she could think about was how she let her grandmother, the children of Beautiful Eyes and the church down. Her head had been too stuck in the clouds to properly prepare. She always properly prepared. But this time, she'd been careless. She was never careless. But then she listened to everyone and decided to get lost in this season, get lost in love and because of that, children might lose their homes and her family's name would be tarnished.

The talking and murmuring was getting to her. The voices of

the men in the room sounded a hundred times louder than she knew they probably were. The television echoed. Her vision started to blur, and she placed a hand on her forehead and leaned into the wall. Salma was the one that noticed her first and walked over.

"Has it started again?" she whispered.

Yasmine nodded.

"You're stressing, that's why. Stop this. There was no way for you to know this was going to happen. I know you; you're in your head beating yourself up. Please don't sabotage your second chance at happiness," Salma pleaded in a hushed whisper. Or at least what she knew to be a hushed whisper because to her, it sounded like she was speaking through a blow horn.

"The weather isn't my fault, but I should have had a backup plan for the benefit," she responded.

"Well, you didn't. We'll figure something out."

Yasmine could hear her sister, but the room seemed to be moving. She could no longer focus on her. She hadn't had a migraine in a while. And she most definitely hadn't had one that came with vertigo in ages. She placed the index finger of her right hand on her ear to stop it from ringing. She wobbled. Salma held on to her waist.

"Mustafa help me!" Salma screamed.

The last thing Yasmine remembered was hearing chairs being thrown out of the way as she went down and everything faded to black.

"Are you sure she's going to be okay?"

"And when the heck did she start having migraines that cause her to faint? Why didn't she tell me about them?"

Yasmine could hear Kojo firing off question after question in anger laced with worry. He sounded like he was ready to fight. She contemplated whether to open her eyes and bear the brunt of his frustration or lie still.

"Man, calm down," Adeniyi told him. "You shouting in her ear isn't gonna give you the answers you seek."

"Explain that to him, my friend. Because I will knock him out, if he shouts at me again," Mustafa said.

"I'd like to see you try," Kojo sneered.

Omar chuckled. "Y'all are so comical. Big Sis will be okay. This happens when she's seriously stressed out. Do you know how much work she put into this benefit?"

Kojo waved him off. "Man, I don't care about that. I'll come out of pocket for whatever amount she's trying to make. All I care about is her opening her eyes."

Adeniyi laughed. "Bruh, she's been out for less than two minutes."

Yasmine groaned and opened her eyes. *Yeah, this man is crazy. He's trying to donate his life savings because I fainted.*

She looked around. She was lying on the couch in her office and everyone was present except her sister. Her brothers knew what to do, so the room had been darkened. The only light in the room came from the hallway since the door was slightly ajar.

"Please, don't ever do that again." Kojo kneeled before her. "You good? You need anything?"

Yasmine tried to sit up, but he wouldn't let her. "The benefit? What's the weather like? Has it finally moved to Tweedes?" Her eyes drifted from Mustafa's to Kojo's.

"Everything is still the way it was, Yas," Mustafa said, his tone somber.

"Sis, don't worry about it. Superstar over there is offering to pay whatever you need to cancel the benefit. So, you can go home and cuddle up with my niece," Omar teased, soliciting boisterous laughter from Adeniyi and Mustafa.

"*hah? madha?* No, that's not funny." Yasmine tried to get up again, but Kojo wouldn't let her. "Kojo let me up."

"Are you sure? You might need to lay down some more."

"Man, let my sister up," Mustafa said, his voice laced with irritation.

Yasmine shook her head at him. Not often did she see this side of her brother. He gave Salma and her latitude when it came to men. His only rule was to never let a man disrespect or put his hands on them.

Kojo helped her sit up and sat next to her, holding her right hand. She reached over to her phone. It was already three p. m. Right before her eyes, the email from the caterers regrettably cancelling their delivery came through. Soon after, all their phones buzzed. She knew what it was without even looking at her phone. The Mayor of Tweede Kans Cove was sending out an announcement limiting movement. She knew the directive came from the region's capital in Fez.

"Okay, we can't stand around here moping. O, come with me. *ladayna 'ashya' lilqiam biha*," Mustafa said.

He walked over to Yasmine and squatted before her. "Yas, this is your first Christmas home in years. I know how hard you've worked on this. At the same time, I don't need you sick." He stood and kissed her forehead. "Keep your phone with you. I'll call you soon." He dapped Kojo and signaled for Omar to follow him.

"Wait up man, let me go to the cottage and get the guys. We can help with whatever you need," Adeniyi said. He dapped Kojo and Yasmine smiled at him. "No more fainting, sis. I can't handle an irrational Keyz."

"Man, get out of here. I wasn't being irrational. 'Preciate it tho," Kojo responded.

Yasmine stood and walked over to the window in her office. The light flurries of earlier had now turned into heavier snowfall. The snow accumulating on the road, tree branches and bushes made for the picturesque destination postcard but in this moment, she appreciated none of it.

Three weeks ago, her heart was cold. She didn't care about Christmas, neither was she emotionally invested in Beautiful Eyes or in a man with whom she really couldn't see how a relationship could work. She would be stupid to deny her attraction and even love for him, but one thing this experience had taught her was that she could get lost in him. With his help, she had just found herself again, but she wasn't ready to be so consumed by love that her business suffered.

"I'm waiting," Kojo's voice pierced through her thoughts.

She could almost envision the scowl he had on his face, but she didn't turn to see it.

"For what?"

"Waiting for the nonsense that's going to come from your mouth, resulting from the stories you have cooked up in your head."

He had only been around her for two weeks. It was like he picked up exactly where he'd left off all those years ago. How he could peg her so well was scary and amazing. That still didn't mean that what he was saying was true. It might be nonsense to him, but it was real life to her.

"It's not nonsense, KJ." She walked over to him.

He still didn't get up from his seat. Instead he leaned back into the chair and crossed one ankle over his knee. He stretched out his arms across the sofa and raised his brow, challenging her words.

"I heard you tell Salma it's your fault." He shrugged. "So, educate me on how you could've stopped Mother Nature. Or are you so used to being the victim, that it's a natural role for you now?" he asked.

She recoiled. The sting of his words had her leaning on her desk. She folded her arms across her bosom and glared at him, looking for the right words to say. "You're being mean for no reason."

"Nah, Babe. See I know you. And I'm not about to let you sabotage your happiness because it affects mine." He stood and walked over to her.

"I can't stop the weather, you're right—"

"Of course, I am."

Yasmine rolled her eyes at him. His nonchalance was beginning to bother her. "What I meant was, I saw this as a possibility some days ago. I could have made adequate arrangements."

"Why didn't you?"

Yasmine bit her lips. His tone was defensive and even though she wasn't sold on them having a future, she couldn't live without him in her life. Kojo was a master at cutting people off. Truth be told, so was she. If not they wouldn't be apart now.

"Why didn't you?"

Her shoulders slumped in defeat. "I was on the phone with the owners of the only sizable hall we have in town but then..." she met his eyes. "I was pulled away to lunch and I forgot to get back in touch with them. I even forgot to make arrangements for the cooks to use the resort's kitchen." She tried to move, but he followed her. "I can't think with you being so close."

"That's your problem. You think too much."

Her mouth dropped. "What?"

He took a deep breath. "What I mean is you're always over thinking stuff. It ensures that you have control over everything. You've been doing that for years. Come on, Yas," he said.

"We can't all live carefree like you," she fired back.

His face hardened. "Is that what you think I do? Live carefree? I don't, I just live! Life happens to me and I happen to it. You on the other hand, exist! Day by day, you exist and mark the days off of your calendar," he seethed.

She swung her head back. It was throbbing. "Will you lower your voice?"

Yasmine strolled over to her seat behind her desk, sat and opened her laptop. She needed to answer the one million emails she probably had with questions. She also had to call her brothers to get a status, then her grandmother and Ms. Bernadette. She had no time to argue with Kojo. His name wasn't on the line. Hers was. She felt his movement. He leaned on her desk, but like she said before, she didn't have time to argue with him.

Several beats passed and her chair was being pulled. It rolled the short distance to where Kojo was leaned with his legs apart.

"You mad at me?" Kojo cupped her face. "You can't be mad at me on Christmas Eve. It's against the rules."

"Whose rules?"

"Sarbah rules," he whispered, in her ear.

Yasmine snickered. "I'm a DuBois-Arazi."

"Not for long. But I got something for you."

"Christmas isn't until tomorrow. I have a major crisis today." Her face contorted. How could he be so blasé about everything?

"And?"

"Kojo, I have work to do. Can't this wait?" she whined. She wanted to be mad at him. She wanted to blame someone, but she couldn't. She loved him.

"No, it can't." He pulled something from the small gift bag, she hadn't even seen earlier. He gave her the square box and she opened it. It was a charm bracelet. But the charms weren't just any charms. She noticed one of them was a vial filled with sand. One had the number eleven and thirteen carved together, another was of a mother and her child and the last one was a Y and K carved together. Her eyes pooled with tears. She looked up at him.

"Is this..."

"Yes, that's the sand from our cave, the age we were when we met. I have one other charm to put on there, but I'mma hold off for now."

She leaned into the hand he had cupping the side of her head. "Thank you," she whispered.

Kojo pulled her up. Her arms went of their own volition around his neck and his arms snaked around her waist. She looked into his eyes. There was no doubt he loved her. She loved him, too.

"You can never have true happiness always holding on to control. I thought we established the Sovereignty of God over our lives. If things turned out this way, we'll find a way around it. Romans 8:28. All things work together for the good."

"I guess I have no choice but to let go."

"No, you don't let go because you have no other choice. You let go because you trust in God," he corrected. "Do you trust me?"

"Yes KJ, I trust you."

"Okay, you'll get exactly what you desire, but I need you to chill out. I can't have no more fainting spells."

She smiled. "Were you worried?"

"Are you kidding? I nearly came to blows with your brother. I can't believe you didn't tell me about those." He tweaked her nose.

"Ugh, stop that. You get on my nerves with that."

"Yeah, whatever. Give me a kiss. Then I gotta go."

Yasmine studied him. "Kojo, what are you up to?"

"I'm not telling you, but I'm also not leaving here until you give me my kiss."

Yasmine placed a light kiss on his lips. When she tried to move back his hand was at her nape.

"You see I knew you'd try to play me." He nudged her head closer and captured her lips in an earth-shattering encounter.

"Man, I know you're not in here kissing when you have us working."

The voice she recognized as Adeniyi's broke their contact. He leaned against the door beam with his hands in his pockets. A smirk adorned his face. He and the other band members had, in two short days, become like her extended family. After that evening in the cave, she and Kojo were glued at the hip and the guys teased him endlessly. They gave her kudos for whatever it was she did to him.

Kojo leaned his head back and grunted. "Go away, man. Can't you see I'm busy?"

"Not as busy as you're gonna be when you working to pay up," Adeniyi countered.

Yasmine frowned. "Pay for what? Kojo, what are you up to?" Her eyes darted between both men, who kept blank expressions.

Kojo kissed her lips lightly. "I gotta go, babe. Stay calm. I'd tell you to go home, but you wouldn't listen. Salma went to check on the kids with Grandma Olly. She'll be right back."

Before she could say anything else, he left the office with Adeniyi.

# CHAPTER 17

"Everything is set up. I got the feed ready to go and everything the band needs is on standby," Omar said.

Kojo nodded. For the last three hours, he, the band and Yasmine's brothers had set up a makeshift hall in the resort. It wouldn't be able to accommodate the size of the audience for the benefit, but it would be just right for the band to play. Phone lines were set up for donations and a Facebook and YouTube Live would stream. The only thing missing would be people inside the room. But if Tweede Kans Cove wanted a concert, then a concert they were going to get.

"Aye, Mustafa, you made sure the town knows to tune in?" Kojo asked.

"Yeah man, this is the second time you've asked me. I had Salma go to the local television station to place the ad. Yasmine went to the radio station. We good to go live in exactly an hour," Mustafa said.

Kojo walked over to Adeniyi and the other guys. They were in the usual huddle they formed at the beginning of any performance. They had agreed on a medley of traditional Christmas songs mixed with their own original songs. Since only one opening act agreed to brave the weather and be here, the 891 Crew would have to carry most of the three-hour benefit.

"I really appreciate you guys coming together like this. I know it's not the ideal space." Kojo said, patting Adeniyi on his back.

"We're brothers, man. We look out for each other," Ifeanyi the band's drummer said.

"Besides we see how you are feeling the babe," Sijuwade the band's rapper and Adeniyi's brother said.

Kojo laughed. "That's just not some babe. That's my wife. She just doesn't know it yet."

They all chuckled then prayed and for the next several minutes did some vocal stretches and practiced some melodies. Yasmine and Salma entered minutes later, gave last minute instructions for members of the staff and volunteers from the church that would answer the phones. Yasmine had wasted no time in preparing a script they would read from. There was no time to train anybody, but Kojo was more than certain this town could pull it off. Everyone loved Beautiful Eyes.

"Aye man, you still wanna do that song?" Adeniyi asked.

Kojo looked over to where Yasmine stood, giving out directives and just being the all-around boss he loved. "Yeah, I'mma close it out with that."

"Cool."

His phone buzzed and Kojo looked at it again. He took in a breath. This was the fifth time today that Lydia was texting him. He hadn't told Yasmine yet, but since the day of the tree lighting at her house, his ex-wife had been on his neck. He had no idea why.

Kwame let it slip during a conversation with his mom that they had spent the day with Auntie Yasmine. Ever since then, Lydia called or texted him about three times a day. He responded to her inquiry about Kwame and how he was dealing with the snow today. He was dealing just fine. In fact, when he called Grandma Olly earlier, Kwame and Anisa were going to build a snowman later.

What surprised him was that when he later told Lydia that this was where he was taking Kwame for Christmas, she wanted nothing to do with the "ancient small town" as she called it. Funny because she had never been to Tweede Kans Cove and it was far from archaic. But now she knew news about the place before he did, and he was the one in town.

"Thank you."

Her voice was soft and shaky.

Kojo turned around to look at the woman who had so much power over him, even after all this time. She was thanking him, but he would move the world for her if he could. He drew her closer and wrapped his arms around her waist. The room was full of people talking, instruments were being played, but all he saw was her. Yasmine's eyes were lowered. She looked like that eleven-year-old girl with the scraped knee.

"Look at me," he whispered.

She raised her eyes.

"I love you, Yas. Your hurt is my pain. My job is to remove whatever stressors you have in life. I know you can handle yourself, and even if I wasn't here, you would've found a way."

"I'm so surprised at how this came together..."

Kojo kissed her forehead. "Before you fainted on me, your brothers and I were already figuring out a way. I might've been gone for a bit, but Tweede Kans Cove is still my town. I have some clout."

"I should've been stronger instead of panicking. But thank you. I love you too, KJ."

"Where you're weak, I'm strong. There'll be plenty of days when I need your strength because I'll be just as weak."

"Aye, we've got ten minutes to show time. Do you guys need some more time to cake over there or are we doing this thing?" Omar yelled.

The room burst out in laughter. He'd just returned with some of his kitchen staff with appetizers and cold and hot beverages to feed everyone that was volunteering.

Yasmine rolled her eyes at her brother and Omar stuck his tongue out at her.

*Just childish.*

"I'm gonna hurt your brother soon," Kojo said.

Yasmine giggled. "Don't you dare." She rose to the tip of her toes and kissed his lips. "I'll be right over there baby." She walked away to give her sister, who was hosting the event, last minute instructions.

Kojo looked over at the DuBois-Arazis. There was no family he knew that was thicker than they were. They had gone through a lot and to see them now... to see himself now, sent chills through his body and he silently thanked God again. He smiled to himself, remembering when Mustafa picked him up from the airport two weeks ago with Omar. He wasted no time in telling them that he was here for the little benefit, but his main goal was to get Yasmine back. They both gave him the third degree, which he expected. But at the end of the day, he told them his goal was to make her his.

❄

Kojo walked back up to the microphone. For the past three plus hours, they had put on quite a show. The Holy Spirit took over and it was nothing but joy and good vibes. He wasn't sure how much money they had raised, but the phones had rung off the hook. At one point, they had to pause and regroup because the internet connection got jammed. In their haste to put something on, they hadn't thought that using Facebook and YouTube Live made it a global event, not just for Tweede Kans Cove. Thus, instead of a three-hour show, it was going on four, but this was the end.

Kojo sat on the stool with the keyboard in front of him. He looked into the camera.

"Hey y'all, thank you for hanging with us. Thank you for your donations. Y'all show us love every time and the 891 Crew would be nothing without you." He played a melody on the keyboard. "Y'all know I don't normally come to the mic, but this next song is brand new and very dear to my heart. It's called "I Still Promise." He paused. "Oh, before I forget, look out for those African tour dates on our website."

Kojo looked behind at the guys and they followed his melody. Then he began to sing.

*You've radiated through my heart,*
*Since the first day we met,*
*My promise to love you forever,*
*Is not one I regret*
*You're my Christmas dream,*
*My second chance,*
*That I've prayed comes true,*
*You're the love of my life,*
*I still promise to marry you,*
*The love lifted me,*
*Guided me,*
*And showed me the way*
*It provided a blueprint*
*To make the most of each day*
*You're my Christmas dream*
*My second chance*
*That I've prayed comes true,*
*You're the love of my life,*
*I still promise to marry you.*

Kojo repeated the chorus a few more times looking at Yasmine. She was leaning on Mustafa and had tears in her eyes. He meant every word he uttered from the deepest part of his soul.

"That's it, folks. Thank you for being here. I thought the views would decrease as the night went along, but they only increased. God bless you and thank you for contributing to Beautiful Eyes. Good night," Salma said.

Omar shut off the feed and the whole room cheered. It was

close to midnight. Yasmine walked over to Kojo and without saying anything, she buried her head in his chest. He held her tight and they remained in silence. No words needed to be spoken as their hearts did all the talking.

# CHAPTER 18

"Good morning, Mummy. It's Christmas. It's Christmas!"

Yasmine groaned, peeping one eye open to look at her daughter bouncing in her bed. It was as though she'd just shut her eyes some minutes ago. Now she was forced to get up.

"Morning, Angel. Yes, it is, but can you please stop bouncing? Mummy will have a headache."

Anisa stopped bouncing and moved closer to Yasmine. She got under the covers and Yasmine smiled. "I'm sorry Mummy, do you want me to turn off the lights and close the curtain?"

"No, my love. It's not that type of headache. Mummy is just tired." Yasmine sat up, leaned against the headboard and pulled her child close. "Merry Christmas, darling."

"Merry Christmas Mummy, I'm so glad we stayed home this year. Can we stay home every year?" Anisa asked.

The excitement in her voice was contagious. Yasmine was glad they'd stayed home this year as well. "Yes baby, we can certainly do that." She picked up her phone. It was a little past seven a.m. After the makeshift benefit the previous night, she and her siblings met Grandma Olly at St. John church for Christmas Eve Mass. When they got there, she had Anisa and Kwame with her.

Kojo and his guys also decided to tag along. Yasmine and Anisa didn't get home until two a.m. But it was now time to get up. Destination: the DuBois Manior.

Two hours later, Yasmine put the last gift in her truck. The roads had cleared up some and the distance to the manior wasn't that far. She walked back into her cottage, pausing at the mirror to check herself out again. Her white cashmere sweater sat perfectly on her waist over her red jeans. She bent down to adjust the zip on her knee length black boots. She wiped the corners of her mouth, ensuring her deep red lipstick wasn't out of place. Fluffing her waves, she smiled.

"Nisa, come on, we're going to be late for breakfast. Mummy is starving." Her stomach growled, confirming that fact. Her daughter came skipping down the hall. She had on a black sweater over a plaid skirt with black stockings underneath. Yasmine adjusted the broach that was crooked and smoothed down the side of her hair.

"You look pretty, my baby," Yasmine said.

"So, do you Mummy." Anisa pulled her hand. "Let's go. Uncle Omar is making breakfast, right?"

Yasmine laughed and locked her door. "What are you trying to say young lady? Don't you like Mummy's cooking?"

Anisa giggled and shrugged. "It's okay, Mummy, but Uncle Omar's is better."

Yasmine shook her head and put her car in reverse. Yeah, she wasn't even going to lie, she was looking forward to her brother's cooking too.

Her family always had Saturday brunch at the Manior. So being around the kitchen wasn't strange for the four of them. But this was different. The joy, laughter and peace couldn't be measured. The family along with Kojo and Kwame had since had breakfast and opened gifts. Omar prepared a light breakfast of a choice between bread or *baghir*, served with jam, honey and butter and his famous mint tea. According to him, the magic would be in dinner. It was noon and prep for dinner was underway. Most of it had been done by her grandmother's kitchen staff the day before. Now, Omar was working his magic.

Yasmine heard the screeching sound of the chorus of "Noel" as Anisa and Kwame put on a concert for Grandma Olly, Ms. Bernadette and some of her other guests in the living room. She and Salma checked on the *bunch de noel*, cake and pies they had put in the warmer. Kojo and Mustafa were mixing the drinks while Omar was doing everything else with the help of Grandma Olly's cook. The aroma was divine and there was music playing in the kitchen as they joked and laughed together.

"Here, drink this." Kojo appeared next to her.

Yasmine frowned at him, then tried to peer into the cup. "Uhmmm, what's that?"

Salma giggled. "Don't do it sis. Next thing you know, you'll be out like a light. Christmas will pass you right by."

Kojo laughed. "Sally, I thought you were on my side?" he asked, then looked at Yasmine. "And you, don't you trust me?"

"Ugh...don't call me that." Salma groaned. "And of course, I'm on your side. I got you here, didn't I? But I draw the line when you got a red cup in your hand."

He laughed. "Okay lil sis, good looking out for that one." Kojo gave Salma a fist bump. "But you know Grandma Olly would kill us if we had alcohol here. So, it's all good."

Kojo lifted the cup to Yasmine's lips and she took a sip. She frowned, but then smacked her lips together. She nodded. "Not bad at all. What is it?"

Kojo kissed her lips. "That's my secret."

"Ooooh, come on guys, not in front of the food," Omar shouted.

"Man, I'm gonna hurt you one day. Why you always hatin'?" Kojo asked.

"I'm not hatin'. Why you always on her? We get you love her, but jeez," Omar complained.

Yasmine giggled. The laughter Omar was trying to stifle slipped through.

"Omar, be quiet and prepare the food. I'm starving with that little breakfast you served," Mustafa said.

"And just for that...watch this." Kojo's hand went to the back of Yasmine's neck and before she knew it, he'd tilted her head back and captured her lips in a deep kiss. One that solicited a moan.

"All right, knock it off," Mustafa said. "I do not wish to see that. Yasmine, go set the table or something so this man can cool down."

Everyone laughed.

"You see that's why whenever I get a man, I'm not bringing him around you guys for nothing," Salma said.

"Ha! Big sis, I can't do too much about, but you, I'mma have a field day," Omar joked. "For all those times you got on and still get on my nerves, it's on."

"Ugh, see why I can't stand you. I don't know how we shared a womb at the same time." Salma rolled her eyes and grabbed Yasmine's hand, leading her out of the kitchen with laughter trailing behind.

How could she be on a euphoric high one minute and less than twelve hours later, it felt like her heart was being ripped out of her chest? Yasmine hugged Kojo tight, her head in his chest while he rubbed her back.

Last evening after Christmas dinner, they all sat down in the family room of her grandmother's house and told stories, jokes and testimonies. Kojo told the whole family of his struggles with alcohol and drugs to ease his pain. He didn't go into detail as he did with her, but he was demonstrating the goodness of God as it related to the season and Jesus. The other members of the band arrived, bearing more gifts and together they sang some tunes *a capella*, watched movies and played games. By late evening, everyone started to disperse.

"Come on, baby. We talked about this yesterday. I would've stayed but I promised Kwame's mother I'd have him back today. Besides, I gotta go prepare for the tour," Kojo whispered.

Yasmine knew he had to leave; she just wasn't prepared for it. It was like *déjà vu* and although it wasn't the same logically, it didn't hurt any less.

"I know..."

Kojo chuckled. "Then what's wrong? You gonna miss me?"

Yasmine looked at him and hit him. "It's not funny."

"Ouch, woman. I'm right there with you. I'm gonna miss you like crazy. But you're coming over before the new year, right?"

"Yeah, I'll try. I ha—"

Kojo shook his head. "Yasmine don't make me act foolish in this airport. You better be in Accra as agreed. I can't go on tour without seeing you."

"Okay, big baby. I'll be there," she said.

His brows arched. "Baby? You're the one that has my shirt wet with tears." He ran his finger through her hair then tugged on it lightly. "Gimme a kiss. I gotta go. I'll call you when I touch down."

Yasmine kissed him and backed away. Kojo kissed Salma on her cheek and proceeded to dap Mustafa and Omar.

"Keyz man, come on, we're boarding," Adeniyi said from the gate. "It was great guys. Thanks for having us." Adeniyi raised his hand and proceeded down the terminal.

"Take care of my wife for me," Kojo said.

"A marriage contract hasn't been signed, so she's fair game," Omar said.

"Mustafa, get your brother. Don't joke with my heart, man," Kojo warned.

Salma laughed.

Mustafa shook his head. "Man, she's good. You better go before that plane leaves."

"I said what I said. Sis, let me see your left hand." Omar lifted her left hand. "Yep, no ring, fair game." He laughed and moved out of the way when Kojo headed toward him.

"Last call for flight 568 to Accra, Ghana," the airline attendant called over the speakers.

"KJ, leave Omar alone. Kwame is with the guys, but he'll be looking for you," Yasmine said.

Kojo walked back over to her. He lifted her chin and stared at her. Love filled his eyes. "You do know you aren't fair game? I'll see you soon." He kissed her one last time and turned to leave.

Yasmine sighed and went to Mustafa who wrapped his arm around her shoulder.

"It's not like before Yas," he said.

"I hope not."

Yasmine knew for certain that if history did repeat itself, she wouldn't survive. And that was not an option. She now had Anisa to consider.

# CHAPTER 19

*I*t'd been two days and he was about to lose his mind. Kojo was on the treadmill in his home gym with his ear buds on. He was on a conference call with the guys and Yetty, finalizing tour dates. He was listening to what was being said, but all he could think about was Yasmine.

When he left and they had their plan to keep in touch, he didn't know it would be this hard. He now knew that there was no way he could survive a year on tour without her by his side. It was a good thing this was their final tour. It had been a great eight-year run. But he needed to shift focus. He had a son who needed him more and a woman he was trying to make his wife, thereby bagging him a daughter.

"Keyz, are you listening?" Yetunde asked.

"Yetty, man—"

"I keep bugging you because I've had to ask you the same question twice," she sassed.

"That's because his mind ain't with him. It's in Tweedes," Adeniyi teased.

"I'm happy you're in love and I can't wait to meet this woman. But I need to handle this with you guys. I have other stuff to do," Yetunde fussed.

"All right, I get it. I'll be in Lagos early January. Can I go now?" Kojo said.

"Yeah, please be on time. Don't make me fly to Accra."

"You don't scare me, little lady. Love you. Bye." Kojo hung up the phone. They had been on the phone for over an hour and he was tired. It wasn't really their fault. He just was in a bad mood.

Hours later, Kojo was showered and in his home studio. He had just finished working on beats for Ziedu Apparel's new promotional advert. The designs embodied every aspect of the Motherland and that's exactly what he relayed in the Afro Beats he came up with. Kojo wasn't done until late in the night. He had a quick dinner and took his tired bones to bed.

He lay with one arm behind his head, facing the ceiling and allowed his mind to wander to his present headache, his son's mother. When they got back from Tweede Kans Cove, he took Kwame back to her. Unfortunately, his son couldn't stop talking about his experience, especially how nice Aunty Yasmine and Salma were.

Lydia knew that it was Yasmine he had an interest in. In the whole time he'd known Lydia, he'd never seen her roll her eyes as much as he did in that one hour he was there. At a point, it irritated him because she was taking the fun out of a time his son genuinely enjoyed.

He pulled her into the kitchen and gave her a stern warning. He made her understand that Yasmine was going to be a permanent part of his life very soon and Kwame would be around her. He recognized she needed reassurance, so he gave it to her. He assured her he wouldn't let Yasmine take her place in Kwame's life, but he wouldn't stop her from being motherly to their son.

He would always have a special place for Lydia. She had given him his son and had endured with him while he wasn't the best man. However, they'd been divorced for years and he demanded respect for his future. Kojo sure did wish she meant it when she apologized and said she wouldn't be any problem.

He picked up his phone and texted.

*Hey baby, you in bed?*
Yasmine: *Not yet. Putting Anisa to bed.*
Kojo: *How's the Angel?*
Yasmine: *Good. She can't stop talking about Kwame. How's he?*
Kojo: *Good. You not gonna ask how I am?*
Yasmine: *I'll Facetime you in a bit.*
Kojo: *Hurry up*

She responded by sending him laughing emojis and a heart.

Kojo passed time scrolling through social media. Minutes later, his phone rang alerting him of a Facetime call. He accepted it and smiled when her face appeared on the screen.

"Hey, you, why are you not in bed?"

"Because I have work to do. Since somebody wants me in Ghana soon." She was seated in her home office with a pencil sticking out of her hair.

"Well then work away."

For the next several minutes they stayed on the phone talking about his day and hers. She informed him that the totals had come in from the benefit and they made three times the amount of money they had anticipated. They went on to give Beautiful Eyes what it needed, and the rest went to their savings fund and the church.

Kojo asked about the Grand Amour resort they had here in Ghana. When he had gotten back, he went to look at the facility. He wanted to know how far it was from his house. It was just about an hour. He knew Tweede Kans Cove was home to her and she had Anisa to consider, but he needed her. He also had no qualms about being selfish about her. Eighteen years was a long time and he wasn't ready to waste another minute.

He had his speech all planned for when she arrived to visit him in a couple of days. For now, the plan was for her to stay for about a week. He looked at the ring on the side of his bed. When he left Tweede Kans Cove, he wasn't sure of when he would pop the question. Being away from her these past few days solidified his plans to do it before the new year. And with any luck, he'd go on tour as a married man. He now saw that he couldn't have it any other way.

Kojo's phone beeped signifying another call coming through. He looked at the screen and it was Lydia. He was going to ignore it, but knew she was out of town and he thought about Kwame.

"Baby, I gotta take this okay. I'll call you back."

"Errr...okay. Love you," Yasmine said.

"Love you, too," he responded and clicked over.

"Hello?"

"Aye Lydia, what's up?" he asked.

"Kojo, it's Kwame."

He jerked into a sitting position. "He all right? What's wrong with him?"

"My cousin just called me. He was playing on the stairs and fell. They are at Alpha Memorial. I won't get there until tomorrow morning," she cried, supplying him with the necessary details.

In a flash, Kojo was out of the bed and changing clothes. Minutes later, he grabbed his keys and headed out.

"I don't know why you're here boring a hole in the carpet instead of on a plane to Accra." Salma walked into her grandmother's closet.

Yasmine sat on the bed. "I'm not supposed to be there until the 31st. That's still two days away."

"Okay, so wait for your perfect little time to go and see about your man who hasn't answered your calls in over twenty-four hours after saying he'll call you back."

Yasmine stood and started sorting the clothes they thought their grandmother should donate. Every end of the year, they went through her closet and purged it.

She sighed. All night she couldn't sleep, waiting on Kojo to call her back. He never did. She woke up the next morning and called repeatedly. The whole day, each call rang and went to voicemail. Then it started going straight to voicemail. Now was the second day and she still hadn't heard from him. She would've called his friends but hadn't thought to get any of their phone numbers.

Salma walked over to her. "Yas, I know that it's in your nature to be careful. You took on the mommy role for us being the first daughter and all. Even though we had grandma and grandpa, you and Mustafa have always taken care of O and me. I get planning and everything, but sometimes you have to put yourself out there. I'm so proud of you for opening your heart, but go check on your man. There's nothing wrong with that."

"She's right, you know." Grandma Olly said, entering the room. "I raised you girls to be strong and independent. I thank God you're both book smart, but I also want you to use your common sense."

"Grandma, are you calling us dumb?" Salma clutched her imaginary pearls.

"Not all the time. But take your sister here – that man pulled heaven and earth to put that benefit together. He loves you, but you will let the fear of the past paralyze you from giving too much of yourself away by popping in on him."

"Grandma, that's not it. It's only been a little over twenty-four hours," Yasmine defended.

"Since he left, how many times a day did you talk to him?"

Yasmine shrugged.

"Too many to count, huh?" Grandma Olly pushed Yasmine's hair behind her ear. "My dear, don't forget reciprocity in relationships is vital. You have the money and the resources to do a round trip if you want to. Don't let fear of the unknown keep you bound."

Yasmine remained silent. There was nothing more to say. She was scared. The idea that this was him cutting her off again was the first thought that came to mind. Then he was a celebrity. For the two weeks he stayed in Tweedes, he was just Kojo, but now back in his world, he was Keyz. True, not stepping outside of the norm and going to Ghana unannounced was her way of maintaining some semblance of control. She dialed him again and still got the same response. None. She disconnected the call and made another one.

# CHAPTER 20

"Lydia, I told you I got it." Kojo said again, as he took a sleeping Kwame up to his room in his house.

It had been a rough forty-eight hours. Kwame had to have minor surgery before they could put his hand in a cast and Lydia's flight from Abuja got cancelled. So instead of him being there for only a couple of hours, he was in the hospital all that while and without a phone. He'd jumped out of bed so fast that night he forgot his phone when he flung it on the bed to get dressed. The minute he got in his car, he knew it wasn't on him, but he thought he'd be away only a couple of hours.

"Okay, sorry. I don't know why you don't want me to carry him home," she whined.

Kojo ignored her and put their son in the bed and covered him with the comforter. He ushered her out of the room and walked into his room to find his phone.

*Of course, it's dead.*

He placed it on the charger with Lydia hot on his trail. He needed her to get going so that he could take a shower and get some sleep. He thought about Yasmine and knew she'd kill him. She was coming in the next day, so he'd make it up to her. But then he knew who Yasmine was and a dull ache passed over his chest. She probably had been trying to reach him, couldn't, and would cancel her trip without a second thought.

*Yas better not play with me.*

"Kojo, I'm talking to you!"

"Lydia, I'm tired. I was already on my way back home when you touched down. I wasn't going to turn around and head to your house. So, I told you to meet us here."

"Okay, but I want him to see me when he wakes up. So, can I at least stay here?"

Kojo leaned against the stair rail and brushed his hand across his face. Lydia wasn't a bad person and he knew she loved their son deeply. He was going to take Kwame to her house in the morning anyway. What harm could it do? He was once married to the woman after all.

"All right. You can take one of the guestrooms. There are extra towels and toothbrushes in there. And I'll drop you guys off tomorrow after breakfast," he said.

The smile that appeared on her face made him chuckle. "I don't know what you're smiling for. You're leaving early...very early in the morning. And since you're here, put your cooking skills to use. I'm starving."

"Only because you were nice." She walked down the stairs while he continued to his room.

Once he got there, he picked up his phone, with the little juice it had, he dialed Yasmine. There was no response. He placed the phone back on the charging pad and went to wash the last two days off his body. Several minutes later, walking back into his room, Kojo rubbed the towel across his hair to soak up the excess water. His stomach growled at the aroma coming from downstairs. Having Lydia at his home wasn't ideal, but his stomach couldn't care less. He dressed, walked over to his charging pad and picked up the phone. He dialed Yasmine again. As had been the case since he'd gotten back, there was no response. His eyes darted to the timer on his dresser and it read eleven p.m. With Morocco being an hour ahead of Ghana, there was no way she wouldn't be

in her bed or getting ready to turn in. There was a strong chance
that she was upset with him, but he would hope not enough to
leave his calls unanswered. He sent her a text.

**Call Me**

Tossing the phone on his bed, he walked to the door. On
second thought, he retraced his steps, picked up the phone and
left the room to calm his roaring stomach down.

"Good morning, Daddy," Kwame yelled once Kojo
entered the kitchen.

"Good morning, buddy. How are you feeling?"
Kojo kissed his son's forehead and made his way to the coffee pot.

"I'm fine, Daddy. See, Mummy drew some hearts on my hand
thing." He showed Kojo his cast.

"It's called a cast, son, and it looks great." Kojo absently
opened the cabinet and retrieved his mug.

"Well, hello to you too," Lydia said, placing scrambled eggs on
a plate and handing it to Kwame.

"My bad. Good morning," he murmured.

There was nothing good about the morning. Or the night
before, since he'd barely slept a wink. But Lydia wasn't to blame
for it. As exhausted as he was, he couldn't get a restful sleep. All
because of a certain, stubborn Arabian woman. The one he knew
he couldn't live without, but who drove him crazy at the same
time. He had tried to call her all night and didn't get so much as a
text cursing him out. Anything but complete silence would've
made him feel better.

She was supposed to come into Accra later in the day.
However, without hearing from her, he didn't know if she was
still coming or not. In a couple of days, he had to head to Lagos.
There was no way he could go back to Tweede Kans Cove to see
what was up.

"I don't remember you ever being so grumpy in the morning," Lydia said. She offered him boiled plantains with egg sauce, which he declined. "Oh wow. You're not eating either. What's wrong?"

Kojo walked to the other end of the island. "Nothing. Are you guys packed up?"

"Are you chasing us?" Lydia took a bite of her toast.

Kojo looked over at Kwame who was busy admiring his cast. He looked back over at Lydia and narrowed his eyes. "Stop it. You know the deal and I'm not in the mood."

She always had a sneaky way of making him look like the bad guy in front of their son. She knew that even though Kwame was adjusting to the divorce, he would love them to get back together. Lydia still used every opportunity she could to put him on the spot in front of their son.

Lydia raised both hands in surrender. "Okay, I was only joking."

"Not in front of him."

The rest of the meal was eaten in semi-silence with Kojo occasionally checking his phone to see if he had any messages. Soon after, everyone was done and Kojo helped tidy the kitchen.

"Okay, Buddy. I'm gonna take you and mummy home now. Go check your room. I think that Avengers toy you said you misplaced is there," Kojo said, helping Kwame down from the stool.

"Okay, Daddy. You'll call me later, right? I want to talk to Aunty Yasmine."

"Sure. She'd love to talk to you as well."

"Really?"

"Yeah, of course. Didn't you have fun with her in Tweedes?" Kojo asked.

"Yeah I did but yesterday, she didn't talk to me, only Mummy." Kwame frowned.

Kojo was about to correct him when there was a shattering sound behind him. He strode to the other side of the island and saw the cup Lydia used for coffee on the floor in pieces. His eyes rose to meet hers. The look on her face was one he would never forget, and he'd always hated. Guilt. What was she hiding?

Kojo looked back at Kwame. "Buddy, you said Aunty Yasmine didn't talk to you yesterday."

"Yes, Daddy. I woke up to pee and heard her talking to Mummy. Before I could come back to talk to her, she was gone."

"Kwame, go upstairs and get what your Daddy told you to get. Let's go," Lydia said, her voice shaky.

"Okay Mummy."

Kojo watched his son turn and run up the stairs, totally oblivious to what was going on around him. Kojo lowered his head and closed his eyes. He tried to control his breathing and the rage rising within. His hands began to tremble, then clenched on their own accord. He shoved them into his pockets, afraid of what he might do. He would never raise a hand to any woman, but he felt like breaking something. That part of him he wouldn't allow his son to witness.

"Please tell me you didn't." His tone was low. Kojo couldn't bring himself to look at her.

"Kojo, wait...I was going—"

"When did she come and what did you say to her?"

"I didn't want to disturb your shower and—"

"WHAT DID YOU SAY TO HER?" Kojo roared. He lifted his eyes to look at Lydia.

"Kojo, Kwame is here..."

Kojo took hurried strides to where she was standing. She tried to move, but he was faster than she was. "I won't ask you again. What did you say to her?"

Her eyes danced back and forth refusing to meet his. She shrugged. "I just told her that you were in the shower and she could wait for you if she wanted to. It wasn't that big of a deal."

Kojo thought back to the previous night. When he came down to dinner, Lydia was fidgeting. He attributed it to anxiety over Kwame. His hand went to his head when he remembered what she had on. If Yasmine saw her, he was officially a dead man.

"Daddy, I'm ready," Kwame screamed from the living room.

Kojo looked at Lydia. Furious would be an understatement to describe how he felt, but he needed to get her out of his house and figure out how to do damage control.

"You go to church, but being this deceitful, there's no way you pray to God. So, you better start praying to whatever it is you pray to that I can fix this. If not, Accra won't contain you and me," Kojo seethed.

He picked up his keys, took Kwame's hand and headed to the door. His brain was in overdrive, trying to figure out where Yasmine would be. If she came that late, she wouldn't have been able to go back to Tweedes already. The Grand Amour in Accra wasn't yet habitable, so she wouldn't have stayed there. He glanced at the time. Based on his calculations, she had had about twelve hours to think the very worst about him. He knew Yasmine well and this was a disaster.

# CHAPTER 21

"No, I'm done taking advice from you," Yasmine said into the phone.

"You mean you're just going to turn around and come home?" Salma asked.

"That's exactly what I'm saying. As soon as the pilot can make his way back." Yasmine pulled out green pants and a floral green and pink blouse from her still packed suitcase.

"I still can't believe the Kojo we spent Christmas with would be that...I don't even have the word."

Yasmine sat on the bed. She ran her fingers through her hair. Her lips quivered and she struggled to keep her tears at bay. It happened again. Christmas had ripped her heart in two. This time however, she'd walked into the trap eyes wide open. So there was no one to blame but herself.

She hadn't slept a wink since she left Kojo's house the night before. She was worrying over someone who had another woman in his kitchen, answering his door in nothing but a t-shirt and shorts. That wasn't how she envisioned coming face to face with Kwame's mother. The woman was gorgeous. Yasmine was still processing her encounter with Lydia. She seemed nice, but Yasmine could tell that she still held a small torch for Kojo. All the assurances Kojo had given her about his relationship with the mother of his son crumbled in that moment. Unlike eighteen years ago, she had a business to run and a daughter to care for. She couldn't afford to shut down, although all she wanted to do was curl up in her bed and cry to her heart's content. But that would have to wait. She had a meeting to attend at the site of the new Grand Amour. After that hopefully, their family pilot would have made his way back and she would be headed home.

"Yasmine!"

"What? Why are you yelling?"

"I have a sister whose heart is broken and I'm not there and she suddenly goes quiet on the phone. I'm worried about you."

"Sal, I'm okay."

"No, you're not. You love that man and for once I wish you would fight for what you want."

"Didn't I just tell you I'm no longer taking advice from you?" Yasmine sighed. "Look sis, we all can't have happily ever after. I had my semblance of it with Pierre. I'm good, or rather I will be." She took in a breath, then exhaled. "When Kojo left all those years ago, I fought for us. I fought for him to stay in my life. Some things are not meant to be and should be left alone."

"But—"

"No buts. Based on your advice, I reopened my heart to him. And I also popped up here only to be met with another woman. That woman had on a Tweede Kans Cove t-shirt – which I'm sure he bought her – and some shorts. She looked way too comfortable in his home. I'm done, Sal."

Several beats passed between the sisters, each one in their own thoughts.

"I'm sorry, Yas."

"No need to be. I have to prepare for this meeting at Grand Amour. You did make sure the pilot was on his way back?"

"Yes, the minute I got your text last night I sent him a message to stay in Marrakech so he can head back out to Ghana this morning."

"Okay sis. I love you. Please don't say anything about this to the guys or Grandma Olly. I'm not ready to hear them plot his death, neither am I ready for grandma's questions."

"Got it. See you later."

Yasmine walked to the hotel's bathroom. She looked at her reflection in the mirror. The tears she held at bay with rage, anger and disappointment cascaded down her cheeks. Her mother couldn't find true love, and it probably was never in the cards for her to find it either.

❄

Kojo paced his living room. It had been five hours and still he was no closer to finding Yasmine than he had been when he dropped Kwame and Lydia off earlier. He tossed his phone from one palm to the other, thinking. He knew she wasn't staying at Grand Amour, but he had made the drive there. No sign of her. She had never been to Ghana before, so there were no spots he knew she would hang out. In all their talks, they never discussed where she would stay when she arrived. The plan was, he'd pick her up and they'd figure out the rest. So, he had no clue where she would've lodged.

Kojo then thought she'd probably gone back home to Tweede Kans Cove. He highly doubted it, but just to be sure, he called Grandma Olly. He had called Salma and got her voicemail. Calling her brothers wasn't an option. They'd know something was up and he wasn't ready to deal with them. Grandma Olly was so elated that he and Yasmine had finally gotten it together. The older woman even made him promise to tell Yasmine to call her after she rested. He couldn't bring himself to tell her that her granddaughter had gone ghost because of him.

He walked to his sofa and plopped down. With his forearms on his knees, he lowered his head. Kojo stayed in that position for several minutes praying to God to help him out. His phone chirped.

Baby Sis Sally: *I can't believe your nerve.*

Kojo's heart thumped against his chest. *Thank you, Jesus.*

He didn't waste time responding via text. He dialed. The phone rang continuously. "Come on Salma. Please pick up," he muttered to himself. She didn't. And his call rolled over to voice-mail. He dialed again.

"What?" she asked on the third ring.

"Where's Yas?"

"Why? So you can finish stomping on her heart?"

Kojo tugged on his beard and let out a frustrated breath. "I know you know that there has to be another side to what she told you. If not, you wouldn't have reached out to me."

"How could you do that to her?" Salma's tone was laced with disappointment.

He'd love to placate her, but he needed to get to Yasmine first. "Sis, I didn't do anything but be nice to the mother of my son." He rubbed the back of his neck. "Look, I'd love to explain further, but your sister has had that vision in her head for more hours than I care for. Can you please tell me where she is?"

"You're saying there's nothing going on between you and Kwame's mother?"

"Nothing at all. I promise. Kwame had an emergency. She came to the house so late that it was just easier for her to stay. I woke up first thing in the morning and took them home. That's all."

He heard Salma take a deep breath, contemplating whether he was telling the truth or not. "Salma, please! You have to believe me. Please tell me where she is." Kojo couldn't keep the begging out of his voice.

Silence for a few minutes then, "It's gonna cost you."

"Name it." Kojo let out a big sigh of relief. He would pay any price to get Yasmine back.

"I want tickets to your next concert."

"Done."

"VIP tickets for me and two of my girls."

"I said done."

"I also want that Ziedu design you were rocking while you were here."

"Done."

"You didn't even ask my size?"

"Salma!"

"Okay, okay, jeez. I'm not the one that told you to have a half-dressed woman in your kitchen."

Kojo winced. He had been right, Yasmine saw Lydia's scanty outfit. He was a dead man. "Sis, you gonna hustle me when I'm down?"

"I got your back, but this is prime info I'm giving you because you know my sister, I'll probably be dead if she finds out I reached out to you. I might as well leave this earth in designer clothes."

"That you can afford…"

"Yeah, but why should I spend my money when you messed up and can afford it?"

"Salma tell me where your sister is," Kojo pleaded again, his voice sterner. He understood he was at her mercy, but she was making his job difficult with each passing moment.

As she talked, Kojo picked up his keys and dashed out of the house. With the phone secure between his shoulder and ear, he put the car in reverse.

"I was at Grand Amour earlier. The guy I talked to didn't even act like they were expecting her."

"Hmmm. Well good luck."

Kojo tossed the phone on the passenger seat and put his foot on the pedal to shorten the one hour drive. Salma said Yasmine was leaving soon. He needed to catch her before she did.

Forty-five minutes later, Kojo brought his car to a screeching halt in the parking lot of Grand Amour. He got out of the car and sprinted into the building. He looked around and the place seemed as empty as it was when he came by earlier. He knew Salma wouldn't lie to him, so he walked toward the back offices. As he approached the hallway, he heard another exit door slam shut and the locks engage. Kojo turned and ran back out through the front where he saw Yasmine walking toward a car on the other side of the building.

"Yas! Yasmine," he yelled. He knew she heard him but refused to turn around. Instead she opened the back door of the Mercedes Benz truck.

"Yasmine DuBois-Arazi, if you enter that car, we're going to have some very real problems," he threatened.

He saw her freeze and was glad she heeded his warning. He was tired, hungry and he really wasn't in the mood to be played with. He got to the car door and closed it. He touched her shoulder and felt her recoil. That stung.

"So, you were really going to leave?"

"What was I supposed to do?" she asked, refusing to look at him.

"If it were me, and I walked in on a man in your house, I'd beat him up, then ask questions," he joked.

Her eyes widened.

"Yeah I know that's not you baby, but you should've waited to see me and demand answers."

"I called you endlessly. No response. Then I come to check on you and there's a woman in her night clothes, cooking dinner," she said, her voice shaky.

Kojo lifted her chin with his hooked finger. "When you say it like that, it is terrible, but I can explain. Still you shouldn't have left."

For the next couple of minutes, he explained to Yasmine the reason behind their communication breakdown and why Lydia was at his house. Quickly adding he dropped them off a while ago. However, he decided it wasn't the time to tell her he only found out some hours ago she was even in town. He needed to get Yasmine back and revealing Lydia's deceitfulness wasn't gonna cut it.

"How is Kwame?" she asked.

"He's good. He can't wait to see you."

A faint smile spread across Yasmine's face. But as quickly as it appeared, it faded. "Does she stay over often?"

Yasmine had never questioned him before. Throughout his stay in Tweedes, she took everything he said about his relationship with Lydia and trusted him totally. He hated that he now gave her a reason to doubt him.

"Yasmine, I love you like I have never loved another. Yesterday was her first time staying in my house. When I built the house, we were already divorced. You're going to be the first and last queen of the castle," he said.

"You scared me."

"I know. I'm sorry, baby. Let's go back to the house."

She raked her fingers through her hair. "Errmm, I was on my way back home."

"Tell the pilot to leave. Or he can stay in Accra. But you're not going back home."

Yasmine's brows creased. He could tell she wanted to argue but he needed the whole fiasco behind them so they could enjoy their time together as planned.

"Have mercy on me. I've been on the go for two days. I need rest, food and my woman." Kojo looked in the car. "Is your stuff in the car or the hotel?"

"The hotel near here. Why?"

"We need to get you checked out and move you closer to me or in with me. There's plenty of room." Kojo tapped on the car and the window came down. "Aye man. You can go."

"Kojo, I'm okay where I am," Yasmine said.

"You might be okay, but I'm not. I can't have you this far away."

Negotiations were over. He took her briefcase, grabbed her hand and led her toward his car. That was a close call. Now that it was over, he was ready to bring the new year in right.

*A* little over an hour later, with her luggage in the car, Kojo drove through the streets of Accra to his house. Yasmine leaned her head back against the leather seat as her mind wandered to the whirlwind of events of the past three weeks. The riot of emotions of the last several hours, almost became too much to handle. Now, she was determined to push the ugly start to her trip behind her and enjoy the next couple of days. She smiled.

"I hope I'm the reason for that big grin on your face?" Kojo asked.

"Nah, it's one other man whom I've known since I was eleven, loved since I was sixteen, ripped and tore my heart into pieces over several years, but has put it back together so beautifully."

"Would it make your smile wider if said man reminded you how deeply sorry he was, that it wasn't intentional and thanks you for giving him another chance? And promises to make it up to you for the rest of his days?" Kojo parked in front of his house and came around to help her out.

"Yes, that would make my smile wider."

He kissed her lips. "Let's go in. I'll get the luggage later."

"KJ, I'm not staying with you."

"It's only for a couple of days, and I'll be on my best behavior." Kojo drew her to him and kissed her again.

"If that's a preview of your best behavior, then it's a firm no from me." Yasmine chuckled. "We need to find another hotel."

"I had to try." He shrugged. "Anyway, while you were packing up, I booked you in another hotel closer. Now woman, let's go inside."

With their hands intertwined, they walked side by side up the short stairs. They entered and she got to see the beauty she'd missed the night before. Kojo took off his hat and the dark glasses he used to hide who he was. When she teased him about them earlier, and he'd told her the reason why, it dawned on her that she was really stepping into that world dating him.

"All this space for just you?" she asked. "You're really on a whole other level. *Je ne sais pas si je peux continuer.*"

"*Arrête ça.* Stop it." Kojo walked back over to her and took her hand. He drew her near the couch and leaned on the back of it. "Yas, my world isn't a piece of cake. It's sometimes very open for public scrutiny. For the most part, I've done a good job of keeping my personal life out of the spotlight. It's quiet now because of the holidays, but I'll be back on tour soon. As much as I want to keep you away, call me selfish, but I can't do life without you. Not anymore."

He took a breath. 'I'll protect you and Anisa as I have Kwame with my life, but that life would mean nothing if you don't share it with me." He moved her back a bit and got on one knee. Yasmine's heart raced. She was expecting a proposal but not now, and definitely not after the way the trip began. One hand went to her mouth.

"Yasmine Camille DuBois-Arazi would you do me the honor of sharing my life with me? Marry me." Kojo reached into his pocket and brought out the most beautiful princess-cut diamond double framed ring she had ever seen. It wasn't flashy, just her style.

She looked down at the man she'd never stopped loving. In two weeks, he'd fulfilled all the promises he ever made to her.

"Yes. Yes, Kojo, I'll marry you," she whispered.

Kojo placed the ring on her finger and gathered her in a sweeping kiss. The Christmas season had indeed been good to her. This memory had single handedly replaced all the bad ones. She blessed God for putting people in her life that forced her to hope.

*Christmas-4: Yasmine-Infinity*

**The End**

# GLOSSARY

<u>French/ Arabic Translations</u>

Although Tweede Kans Cove is a fictional town, it is located in Morocco. Therefore, the culture of Morocco is threaded in the story. Moroccans speak Arabic and French mainly. However, with foreign influences, English is also spoken to some extent. Below are translations (done to the best of my ability) to the languages I used in the story. I have this in the order in which they appear

*Je t'aime aussi* : I love You too (French)

*Écoute mon enfant:* Listen my child (French)

*hal tasheur baltjahl* : Are you feeling left out? (Arabic)

*Je sais où la chercher* : I know where to look (I know where to get her (French)

*tueal wamishi maei* : Come walk with me (Arabic)

laqad qult lak dhlk edt marrat : I've told you that several times Arabic)

*Vrai* : True( French)

*Tu comprends:* Do you Understand (French)

*Oui je comprends* : I Understand (French)

*Vraiment? Depuis quand:* Really? Since when (French)

*Hein?* huh? (French)

*la tahzan:* don't be sad (Arabic)

*kayf hal tifli:* How is my baby (Arabic)

*'ayn tuqimin allayl:* where are you staying (Arabic)

*madha qult:* what did you say (Arabic)

*ymkn 'an tajealak tasheur bitahasun:* does that make you feel better (Arabic)

*la tabda maei :* don't start (Arabic)

*'ana ahbik ya 'ukhti.:* I love you sister (Arabic)

*hah? Madha :* huh? What? (Arabic)

*ladayna 'ashya' lilqiam biha :* we have things to do (Arabic)

*Je ne sais pas si je peux continuer:* I don't know if I can continue (I don't know if I can keep up (French)

*Arrête ça :* stop it (French)

# FINAL NOTE

Thank you for reading Yasmine & Kojo's story and the introduction to the DuBois-Arazi family. Please consider leaving a review on the platform you purchased the book. I greatly appreciate honest feedback. They really go a long way. The number of reviews a book receives greatly improves how well it does.

If you liked this story, I trust you might like some of my other titles. But before we get to those, never miss a sale, new release announcements, or freebies. You can ensure that by joining my mailing list. I'd love to stay connected.

Next up in the DuBois-Arazi family is Mustafa DuBois-Arazi in Destiny Fulfilled. You can get it here.

# AN EXCERPT: DESTINY FULFILLED

Zaina decided to create distance between them. She turned and tried to move away but Mustafa grabbed her arm. He pulled her closer to him, a feat she didn't think was possible with how close they were already. Her eyes moved from their point of contact back up to his eyes.

He loosened the grip on her hand and bent toward her ear. It was only the two of them in the room, so he didn't need to whisper but being so close to her neck was a power play.

He remembered her spot.

"Don't flirt with my staff to get a reaction out of me."

Zaina shook him off. "Then don't try to police who I can and cannot spend time with."

"You're not allowed to spend time with my staff outside of business." He shoved his hands into his pockets.

"Not allowed? Are you kidding me?"

"You know I don't kid."

"It must be something new for you because you can't be serious."

Mustafa stared at her for a few second then sauntered to the door. "It will be in your best interest to heed my warning." He threw over his shoulders.

She was so frustrated with this man that she wanted to scream. Of course, she wasn't going to date anyone while she was here. But what made him think he had a say in what she did? He didn't want her but was upset that somebody else did. This was part of their problem, communication. She wasn't going to go with the flow anymore. Mustafa placed his hand on the doorknob when Zaina decided to try one last time.

"Musa!"

He froze but didn't turn around. She continued.

"For the millionth time. I'm sorry. But this is where I draw the line. You can't have it both ways. It's clear you don't want me, but you can't dictate who does."

He turned. His fiery eyes roamed her body before landing on her face. "People here have families to feed or people who depend on them. I'll hate for you to be the cause of them losing their jobs."

Her brows came together. "You wouldn't."

"Try me."

"Ugh!! I can't believe you."

"Believe it *Chérie*."

His eyes dared her to challenge him, but she was stuck on the French term of endearment he used for her. She was painfully aware that nothing about this moment was endearing but to hear it come out of his mouth was something she longed many nights for. Zaina was tired of fighting with him. She had to think of a way that she could monitor the work from Gaborone and come to the resort once a week. This wasn't going to work for her. She had done a lot of work to get to where she was mentally and emotionally. Too bad, he hadn't done the same.

Order Here

# ALSO BY UNOMA NWANKWOR

**Stand Alone Books**

*An Unexpected Blessing*

*He Changed My Name*

*When You Let Go*

**The Ultimatum Series**

*The Christmas Ultimatum*

*The Final Ultimatum*

**Sons of Ishmael Series**

*A Scoop of Love*

*Anchored by Love*

*Mended with Love*

*Redeemed Through Love*

*Mixed Tidings*

**The Invisible Shackles Series**

*To Live Again,*

*To Breathe Again*

**The DuBois-Arazi Family Novels**

*A Promise Fulfilled*

*Destiny Fulfilled*

**The Billionaire Pact**

*Vegas Nights*

*Second Shot*

*Pretend Bae*

**Away To Africa**

*New Year's Kiss (Prequel)*

*Rent-A-Bae*